Scatter My Ashes At Tur

Sara Llewellyn

Published by
Sara Llewellyn,
2023

Scatter My Ashes At Turtle Creek

By Sara Llewellyn

SCATTER MY ASHES AT TURTLE CREEK

Chapter One

Driving down the Welsh mountain road, in a Mini Clubman Estate with a large wardrobe strapped to the roof rack, was all in a day's work for Seph Cody. A clap of thunder prompted her to count out loud until another flash of lightning electrified the heavy grey sky. The torrential rain and gale-force March wind didn't unnerve her, it satisfied her fatalistic frame of mind that morning, even when she was compelled to brake hard as the heavy furniture almost took off with the car suspended underneath by the creaking roof rack. 'Oh no you don't .. I drilled those bolt holes myself, it's going to take more than a storm ..' The back wheels left the ground before landing again with a bump. The hedgerows towered either side of the steep narrow road, their branches clattering against the sides of her car and the next thunder-clap sent a wild, skittish buck deer leaping from the bank, just missing Seraphina. The animal's impact, had it come crashing onto the windscreen, would have killed her instantly. Her emergency stop stalled the engine and instead of thanking her lucky stars that she wasn't dead, Seraphina got out of the car and defiantly looked skyward soaked to the skin now, and shouted, 'Missed …You Bastard!' Her innocent faith in a benign God had been undermined lately.

Seraphina Trinity Cody, or Seph as she was known, had gone up into The Welsh Valleys that stormy day to do business with a couple of furniture dealers, which she'd been doing on and off for years, rain or shine. She looked forward to the visits because she and the dealers were old friends now and they usually had a hilarious time, bargaining ruthlessly and spinning one tall tale after another about the things they were buying and selling. Seph was a good customer and whenever she made the call to say 'I'm coming up', all hands were on deck. 'Come on boys! Get that shipment from France unloaded, now! Seph Cody's coming up!', Neil the owner of the vast warehouse, would shout. Next Cath, his wife, would get cracking and without taking a breath she'd rattle off the orders. 'Right then, I want all the good armoires over there, where she can see them properly. Unload the Salon Suite with the big Pier Glass and put the buffets and dining tables nearer the front. Candelabras! Get them all out on the tables and put the upholstered Louis armchairs under the window, in the light, to show off the brocade …. that's it. Oh! The Paris clocks. Make sure they're displayed and wind a couple of them up, so that they chime when she's here … you know how Seph can't resist a pretty chiming clock.'

But the usual irreverent joking and laughing that went on whenever Neil, Cath and Seraphina got together, was subdued that rainy day. The warm greetings and hugs were quieter and more meaningful – they hadn't seen Seraphina for a long time and had heard of her sad news. She was struggling inside, and her friends sensed it and were watching out for her, ready to step in and help. Seph was expert at choosing the right stock for her shop, and that day she simply nodded 'yes' to the pieces she wanted. The buying done, Seph and the boys loaded the French armoire on to the roof of her tiny car, a final tightening of the straps was carried out with a professional flourish and experienced know-how by Seph. Arrangements were made for the rest of the furniture she'd bought that day to be delivered to her shop by the end of the week. Against the advice of Neil and Cath, Seph had insisted on taking the armoire herself, in spite of the terrible weather, because she didn't want to let an impatient customer down. Neil and Cath smilingly waved her off, not letting on how concerned they were by their dear friend's heartbreak that was written all over her pale face. Seraphina's unstinting bravado under the circumstances, keeping herself busy, business as usual, was painful to watch. Cath shook her head as Neil put his arm around her, 'She'll be alright .... Just you wait and see ... this is Seph

Cody we're talking about right?', 'Right', sighed Cath.

It was still only mid-morning by the time Seph was safely down the mountain and back at her shop. 'Woah ... steady', she said skidding onto the small gravel car park sounding more like she was stopping a wagon and horses than her battered blue Mini. Running through the bucketing rain and unlocking her shop, she turned the Closed sign to Open. Her answer machine was flashing red with a dozen messages from as many eager customers, all wanting her hand-painted furniture.
'Umm .. nice to be popular' she breezed before picking up the phone and calling Mrs Steeply, 'Hi there it's Seph Cody here, your armoire has arrived.'
'Oh that's marvellous, I'll be over this afternoon to discuss paint finishes and colour.'
'Great, see you then, then', Seph chirped, putting down the phone.
A sale was on the cards, 'Should make a nice little profit, especially if she wants it gilded ... good.'
After a single-handed struggle to unload the dismantled wardrobe and put it all together again for viewing by Mrs Steeply, Seph sat down to catch her breath and go through the morning's post, deftly aiming the junk mail at the big bin, sending it spinning through the air with crack shot precision. She was just about to dispatch

the last thick envelope when she spotted the American stamps and stared at it, frozen. Her eyes moved to the beautifully carved empty mirror frame opposite, half way through being regilded, and she was glad she couldn't see her reflection staring back.

Her long white apron was the backdrop to her trade, almost every square inch of it covered with paint, the handy front pocket contained an old French key, a screwdriver and some sheets of gold-leaf in a small card envelope. The apron ties wrapped twice around her slim waist, over faded, worn Levis piled onto steel toe-capped work boots. A white paint-spattered shirt buttoned to the neck and done up at the cuffs hid her lovely shape, all trussed up under the apron bib. Her blue, usually sparkly, eyes were framed by long dark hair pulled back into a ponytail and tied with an off-cut of soft yellow deer-skin. She wore no make-up or jewellery, her only face decoration that day was a smudge of pale blue paint on the end of her nose. The grey strands in her hair were accidentally painted on. She had strong artists hands, long-fingered and capable.

Seraphina Trinity Cody took a deep breath, vainly trying to calm her churning stomach as she opened the envelope. She knew what was inside and sure enough, though still not quite believing it, she unfolded the Deeds to a ranch in America.

Gabe, her beloved Texan cowboy fiance had gifted his entire 'outfit' to her. The ranch was a surprise wedding present for his soulmate Seraphina, his cherished wife to be. But Gabe had died, and it was only upon hearing the devastating news, that she was told about the ranch. In the blink of an eye her lover's gift made for sharing had become a bequest for her alone. Her shock at seeing what she already knew, in writing, unequivocal, threw her backwards, all the myriad of feelings she had sat on with sheer willpower for months, surfaced one after the other – horror, grief, confusion, then a mingling of amazement and joy before reacting instinctively to the real and longed for prospect of a different life, the one she held in her trembling hand …'Oh Gabe .. you beautiful, beautiful thing ..' His gift kept her connected to him, which was giving her the strength to keep going. 'My god there is a God … there is a bloody God .. thank you dearest Lord', she wept.

Seraphina loved Gabe like no other. For a year the happiest time of their lives was lived and felt, against a backdrop of untouched Texas Hill Country, the environment and landscape described by those in the know as Gods Country. Just him and her and a two-horse trailer, driving and riding and camping and dancing, melting into the dusk under the stars, night after passionate night. Romance so intense, so utterly fulfilling, it became sublime. While she was still clutching the half-read letter, the shop bell jingled and in came a man from Fed Ex with a parcel delivery. She hesitated before signing for it, because it too had come from Texas. The package contained an old, dog-eared book, The Cowboy At Work – All About His Job And How He Does It, by Fay E. Ward, an old hand cowboy's memoirs, written in the late nineteen-thirties. She turned the first page, there was an inscription in Gabe's hand.. 'Seraphina, you never know when you might be needin' this. Love ya 'til I die, Gabe x.' The poignancy was unbearable for Seph, the book was a Christmas present from months ago and Gabe hadn't lived long enough to give it to her, loving her until he died, not knowing he was about to. It was still wrapped in paper with reindeer and tinsel on and had been forwarded to her by Gabe's friend, Chester the Gun. Instinctively she ran her hand over the writing and held back a well of tears. The scent of the absolute love of her life was all around her, out of context in her little shop, thousands of miles off-beam. One slow tear rolled down her cheek and dropped onto the page almost dissolving the G in Gabe.

Being given a working ranch in Texas in the middle of wild, uninhabited Hill Country made her feel like a free spirit. As far back as she could remember she'd had an entirely romantic love of The Wild West and, like millions of other people was fascinated by the whole epic story of ranch pioneers and homesteaders, staking claims in gold-fever mining towns, cowboys and Indians.

That history of America drew her in, she felt like she should have been there. Had she been born in 1869 instead of 1969 she might have been galloping full pelt around a majestic buffalo herd with a curious Indian trotting behind, waiting for her to fall off her side-saddle. Just like her long-lost Welsh cousins before her, she'd barter her precious Welsh red flannel garments for the land-keeper's antlers and buffalo hides.

The shop bell jingled again and her Mum came in to put the kettle on and make a nice cup of tea, which they always drank in her workshop at the back. They perched as usual on whatever filled the space that day. A carved oak dining table, a walnut bench and the dismantled parts of a 19th Century French Buffet. A long trestle table running against the wall carried its usual jumble of restorer's stuff. Tins of wax polish, shellac, a zillion paint colours in different size tins and jars, paint brushes, muslin cloth, candle sticks, tools, boxes of old French hinges and keys, wads of gold-leaf. The walls were plastered with 'To Do' lists numbered 1-37 that day.

'Any 'clecs?' Mum asked.

A 'clec' in a Welsh world means a bit of news, a bit of gossip, something hot. Seraphina gulped back Mum's scalding tea and it sizzled a bit on the back of her parched throat and dry tongue.

'Any news?' Mum asked again, looking directly at the letter still clutched in her daughter's hand.

'Mum, you know the story your Great Grandfather told? The one passed down the generations about us all being looked-out for by the spirit of a dead Indian Warrior Chief?'

'Yes'

'What was his name?'

'White Cloud.'

Her Welsh ancestors were part of the original push West. They jumped on the fabulous bandwagon and emigrated from Wales to America, some working on the railroads. Two brothers in particular embarked on the great bold adventure and awoke one morning to discover they had been visited while they slept under the stars. A strange and equal Santa had taken their precious Welsh red flannel shirts and left in their place a magnificent set of antlers and a buffalo hide, so heavy and thick, that their spindly underfed arms could hardly fluff it out. The Welsh are tribal by nature, it is endemic and inescapable, glorious. So it's no surprise that those Welsh brothers should feel quite comfortable with tribal Indians and relate to them in a fair and square Welsh way.

Seraphina thought she'd never know what went on back then, but something moved the brothers and something moved the Warrior Chief. Seraphina liked believing that even in the 21st Century, the spirit of a long gone Chief named White Cloud was somehow looking after her. She wondered if the story was true or just a bit of good old Welsh family folklore. After all, her Aunty Xantie was always the first to pipe up smiling and twinkling, 'Give lying a chance', with her grey hair in a prim French pleat, demurely sitting by the fire in her retired infant school teacher's outfit.

'And?' her Mum pressed, 'Have a digestive biscuit, is it the wrong time of the month?'

Seraphina shook her head and handed over the letter with the Deeds.

'Gabe's definitely dead Mum.'

'Darling ... I know, try not to go upsetting yourself, you will get through this.' Her mother read the letter out loud with her arm around her daughter.

'Dear Ms S.T. Cody,

We write to you, enclosing the Deeds of Turtle Creek Ranch, which you legally own. As you are aware, Mr Gabe Nathaniel Johnson passed away some months ago. We are extremely sorry for the time matters have taken to clear Probate and send our sincere condolences for your sad loss.

Your property includes 350 acres, a log cabin, a herd of longhorn cows, 5 quarter horses, a pair of mules and a goat named Cricket. The barns and buildings on the estate are also included, as well as an open pick-up truck and horse trailer and various items of farm machinery. At this stage we would appreciate it if you would reply by return, there are papers to be signed and so forth, as well as some pressing matters regarding the welfare of the livestock in your absence.

Yours faithfully, Messrs. Matt Sydney & James Peterson. Probate Lawyers,
Droversville, Texas.'

'Well, well, well.' said Mum.
Perching next to each other, mother and daughter stood up spontaneously and raised their tea and clinked cups. The Toast was difficult – to the memory of the lost love of Seraphina's life and the wonderful gift of the thing she'd always wanted and never dreamed she'd actually get – a ranch in Texas.
Seraphina cleared her throat, fighting back tears, before speaking.
'To Gabe, then.'
'To your lovely, handsome Gabe', smiled Mum, hugging Seraphina and trying not to cry.

Chapter Two

Seraphina and Gabe had been a perfect match and it never ceased to amaze her how they had

met in the first place, the chances being about a billion to one. Yet somehow they did – two people, a giant ocean apart, had found one another.
Seraphina had her Painted Furniture shop in a rather nice little historic Welsh market town, filled with well-to-do people who read glossy design magazines like 'World of Interiors'. Gabe on the other hand was the archetypal cowboy who spent his days outdoors, rounding up cattle. Her shop was a prime candidate for posh magazines, not because she contrived or copied but because she had created a wonderful place selling exquisitely finished, hand-painted antique furniture. The atmosphere in her shop was delightful and even her stodgy bank manager loved it. Clean sawdust on a white painted concrete floor, soft spotlighting and a heady smell of paint and varnish mixed with antique wood and coffee, freshly brewed. Authentic open stone walls, rough wood staircase, black forged bars on the window and stable doors as an entrance. A visual feast and a place you wanted to be – to stay. It was not unusual for a customer to come in and simply sit in one of the beautiful French armchairs and just gaze at the array of painted pieces – armoires, bedsteads, buffets and sideboards, dining tables and chairs and 'bon heure de jours' jostled for some of the spotlight. A sophisticated muted rainbow of colours and gold. On one occasion a man came in and sat down at one of her hand-painted eight-foot-long dining tables and just spread his

arms out, palms down with his cheek resting on the spectacular silk-smooth surface and said in a hypnotic way, 'I must have this table ..' So business was good but intense hard work, Seraphina hadn't had a holiday for years, she was almost burnt out and knew she needed a change of scene. For a long time she'd been wanting to treat herself to a trip to America to see the West, to ride across the 'open range' and to try and experience the life of a cowgirl, to live out a romantic desire to round up cattle and sleep under the stars. So Seraphina chose a holiday in Texas and did the unthinkable thing of closing her shop for two weeks and to hell with the consequences.

She arrived in Bandera, Texas, 'Cowboy Capital Of The World' on Boxing Day, Christmas. It had been a good six years since she'd had any kind of break or fun or recreation, and as for romance well she'd about given up. She'd ridden all her life and was hooked on Westerns so was looking forward to her dream holiday. According to the Ranches-R-Us brochure, all she had to do was 'ride all day and unwind', away from the shop, the telephone, the customers and all that pressure. She was travelling to a place where she could recharge her batteries unknown and unfettered.

It was the day before she'd met Gabe or knew of his existence.

‘Right, how hard can it be to unwind?‘, she asked herself as she stepped off the plane in San Antonio, sailed through passport control and reclaimed her luggage. The drive from the airport was a welcome relief after the long flight and she thought about The Alamo and the legendary siege where every man was brave, a superhero in fact, and all dead. An appalling waste of great guys way back in a different century, when a great guy really was a great guy.
Her chauffeur that day was the ranch owner himself, who had driven from his Running Deer Ranch in the middle of The Texas Hill Country to personally collect his paying guest. When Seraphina booked her holiday she basked in her belief, that staying on a working cattle ranch would be a small adventure, an uplifting, precious fourteen days, and the prospect was already making her feel relaxed and carefree. She was looking forward so much to a glimpse into another world as far away and as different as possible from her life at home in Wales. The ranch owner introduced himself as Marvin and gave Seraphina a warm Texas welcome, ‘Just call me Boss, everyone else does’, he chuckled, courteously carrying her enormous suitcase. The drive from San Antonio flew by, as she listened to Boss, telling her all about the things they were going to do on her visit, ‘Most of it on horseback too‘, he chuckled again. Eventually they left the highway and drifted into the Hill Country itself, a pink sunset ignited the tan-coloured, caliche dirt road, rolling out ahead

with bambi-eyed deer poised along the winding route, threatening to leap right over Marvin's massive cowboy truck. Seraphina was moved so deeply by the stupendous landscape surrounding her, she silently blotted tears from her eyes.

It was dark by the time they reached Running Deer Ranch, Seraphina clambered out of the truck and was directed to a log building with twinkling lights and an enticing aroma of food cooking. She opened the door and was greeted like a long lost relative by Florence the ranch owner's wife. After a delicious Texas size supper and friendly introductions to the other cheerful guests, Seraphina was shown to her own individual log cabin, her home for the next two weeks.

She slept well that first night in Texas and woke early, excited at the chance to actually wear all the fabulous cowboy riding gear her sister had bought for her from a rather nice equestrian outfitters in Marlborough. An Australian Stockman's hat with a very flattering wide brim and a real humdinger of a riding jacket in navy and canary yellow. A Dutch cotton scarf tied in a triangle round her neck with a stencil pattern, like Delft china. Cowboy boots and jeans with pure silk long-johns underneath and a pair of yellow-tanned deer hide riding gloves. She dressed and, as there were no mirrors in her log cabin, hoped she looked the part, which she did.

She stepped out of the cabin and found herself in the most beautiful remote landscape, a Texas Winter wilderness. A slight mist softened all the edges, like a painting in watercolour only more dynamic. Green cedar bushes, huge oak and pecan trees, orange and tan and saffron earth and dirt pushing up to and around hills and rocky bluffs in the distance. She shuddered a little, feeling the December cold on her back, and smiled a little, feeling the warm sunlight on her pale face. The scent of juniper was delightful and invigorating, fresh and hopeful on this gorgeous morning in the middle of nowhere.

Slow footsteps crunched nearer, she turned and looked, as pretty as a picture, straight into the eyes of Gabe, the ranch foreman and head wrangler. He wore a well used Stetson hat and the hat-band was a fine horsehair plait woven with silver beads, which glinted in the freezing morning light. Clean shaven and tanned, his fine bone structure made more handsome by the ruggedness of his complexion, having lived an outdoor life. His pressed blue shirt was patched in two places with faded red material and his forearms were protected with tooled leather cuffs. The cotton scarf tied round his neck and knotted at the front was printed with a faded Texas lone star on frayed lilac. His Wranglers and worn cowboy boots just showed from under heavy dark fringed chaps, the old studs decorating the outside edge were scuffed and battered. His waistcoat was worn leather and a

pair of old iron spurs hung from his belt. A coiled rope swung from his arm.
'Welcome to Texas, Mam, ain't this just a beautiful mornin.'
Seraphina stared unselfconsciously deep into his warm hazel eyes and faltered only when he removed his glove to shake her hand. The warmth of that gesture, that moment, made her acutely aware that for years she had denied herself physical contact with any man, she didn't know why, other than the fact she was always up to her neck in running the business at home, and there simply never seemed to be any eligible men where she'd lived and worked as her life had ticked by. Looking shyly down she tried to remove her new glove to complete their handshake but the small button on the inside of her wrist wouldn't undo. Gabe gently undid it for her and they shook hands. The sensation of feeling his warm skin on the inside of her frozen palm was like a litmus paper soaking up and proving her buried, almost forgotten yearning for intimacy and human need for love. Now, you put a thirty year old woman who hasn't been held and kissed tenderly for years in the middle of the Texas Hill Country with a man like Gabe and you have a recipe for an event. As she sat opposite him having breakfast that first morning, her words of the night before echoed in her mind, 'how hard can it be to unwind?' Now she had the answer – it was as easy as needing something and finally being presented with it. Breakfast was

divine, coddled eggs over easy with delicious thin crispy bacon, which Americans ate with their fingers. Warm baked shiny bagels and blueberry jam washed down with fresh orange juice and rich, powerful cowboy coffee. The scene that morning lent itself to the art of sensual pleasure, Seraphina ate in a different way. A gorgeous, surging attraction orchestrated every luscious mouthful and Seraphina felt she might actually pass out. She just got prettier and prettier and Gabe was ignited - she had his attention.

The other guests, all of them couples, were tucking into breakfast too, and the room was filled with chatter and excitement at the ensuing day's adventure. They were all wearing the necessary garb, boots, jeans, chaps, spurs and carefully chosen cowboy hats in various shapes and sizes. This was the land of scorpions and deadly rattlesnakes and frisky cows with very long sharp pointy horns, not to mention the highly trained all American Quarter Horses who, with one inadvertent squeeze of the thigh, would rear up, sit down, stand on their heads and sing the American National Anthem, all at a full gallop. 'So how do you train these amazing Quarter horses?' Seraphina asked. 'Mam, I'd be mighty pleased to show you, if you're hankerin' after knowin' said Gabe, longing to squeeze her fluttering waist. The way he said 'Mam' made Seraphina tingle all over and almost tumble into wantonness. She found herself blushing as they walked along towards the barn to saddle up and ride out. For years she'd been telling herself that celibacy suited her, that she could spit in the eye of leg-waxing and the bother of keeping a heavenly scented, silk smooth body 24/7. Her unreliable premise, that the longer you go without something, the less you need it, was about to be tested and get well and truly blown out of the water. A love at first sight phenomenon had begun. The intensity and certainty between Seraphina and Gabe, two strangers, changed both their lives forever. The holiday of a lifetime she'd paid thousands of dollars for, proved to be worth every last cent. That first morning, Gabe gently gave Seraphina a leg up into the saddle – as light as a feather, he thought and noted how relaxed and secure she was on her mount, Playgirl, a small helpful Quarter horse. The packed lunches were put in the saddle-bags and off they went. Suddenly, Playgirl started side-stepping and spinning in circles before rearing up. 'Yee Ha!' shouted Seraphina, quite carried away with the happy carefree world she now found herself in. Gabe held his breath and the other guests looked on open mouthed – here was a woman who could ride. Still firmly astride Playgirl and glowing with excitement, Seraphina and Gabe, along with the merry band of wannabe cowboy guests, headed out to the hills. What a day they had, and what joy she felt transported now to another world, a million miles from her shop life in Wales. They set off at quite a pace up hill and down dale, leaping into rivers, hurtling over rocks and getting bashed in the face with tree branches all before they'd even had lunch. The hectic start to the trail ride was not what Gabe had planned, but a rather nice couple from Maryland who normally spent their days running a Dry Cleaning business were wearing souvenir spurs, one's they'd bought at the airport, as sharp as upholstery tacks and not meant for using. So the more they hung on for dear life the deeper the spurs were pressed into their willing Quarter horse's ribs and the faster they went. It was time for lunch and right on cue the runaway horses, Ben and Moby stopped dead causing the couple from Maryland to fly through the air with their spurs still spinning like small propellers. 'Ok folks, time for a break' said Gabe picking the guests up from the ground and dusting them off. 'Are you still in one piece Sybil?' Feeling herself all over Sybil said she was. 'And Leonard how about you?' Panting with rosy cheeks Leonard spluttered 'Yup! Exhilaratin'! That's what that was ... exhilaratin!' Gabe had everyone dismount and when the horses were safely tethered he quietly asked the group if they wouldn't mind taking off their spurs and putting them away. A campfire was mustered and they ate lunch ravenously as Gabe made hot coffee to thaw them out. The freezing December temperature had numbed Seraphina's hands and feet and they were all feeling the painful effects of an outdoor life, however refreshing. Not wanting the sweating horses to get cold Gabe had everyone back in the saddle and on the move again swiftly, 'Sorry folks' smiled Gabe, 'but the horses come first around here.' Everyone overplayed an enthusiastic response to Gabe's orders, not because they weren't having the time of their lives but because they were so saddle sore they could barely stand up never mind walk and climb back on a horse. Leading the troop Gabe signalled with his hand shouting 'Okey dokey let's move on out' The Texas Winter weather was getting blustery and the trees surrounding them were creaking and swaying as they set off spurless, heads bent to the wind with screwed up eyes and chapped lips.

Chapter Three

It was early evening when Seraphina finally climbed off Playgirl that first day, she and the other guests were in pretty bad shape. Happy, but stiff, hungry and freezing cold. Gabe had looked after them wonderfully and knowing how saddle sore they all were, he recommended a session in the hot outdoor Jacuzzi before supper. 'Okey dokey ..great idea', they all mumbled in various states of dishevelment. Everyone staggered back to their log cabins and once inside Seraphina heaved her boots off with extreme difficulty and turned the electric fan heater on full blast. Weakly tearing her clothes off, the final layer of silk long-johns were stuck to the blood of her burst blisters on the inside of her knees. She had a face like a red weather beaten hobo and her hat-hair was flat as a pancake and welded to her skull. '..bloody hell ..no wonder all those sepia photos of ye olde pioneery women show them with leather complexions and granite jaws.'

Still smiling at the wonder of her day, she lit a cigarette and nearly fainted as the nicotine hit her bloodstream. Hobbling into the bathroom she stepped into a hot shower. 'Bliss … absolute bliss..' she burbled through the soothing wonderful warm water, before frantically shaving her legs, exfoliating every square inch of her feminine body and painting her toe nails. Next she and the other guests, only wearing swim suits in the freezing December twilight, gingerly headed for the steaming outdoor Jacuzzi and submerged themselves, bubbling away, watching the divine pink sunset. The sound of tinkling bells, 'jinglebobs', 'danglers', sent a quiver through Seraphina, as Gabe approached, his worn leather chaps and metal spurs shimmering in the gorgeous natural, glowing light. 'Enjoy your dinner folks..' smiled Gabe 'You've earned it .. and I'll see you all in the morning for some more adventure.'

Seraphina, perfectly mesmerized, gazed up at the cowboy who stood before her. Lying in her bed that night she imagined what her life might be with a man like Gabe. The next morning just before dawn, she was woken by a tap at her cabin door. She could see the unmistakable silhouette of Gabe casting a shadow across the window, the shape of his Stetson brim, the straight long stockman's coat and the once-heard-never-forgotten sound of the tinkling jingle-bobs dangling from his spurs. She opened the door, sleepily unafraid. He was tall and had to bend his head without saying a word to kiss her cheek, then her forehead, next the tip of her nose, turning his head to kiss the front of her throat holding each of her arms tenderly and not letting go. Moving his mouth to her ear he whispered, '.. adopt a cowboy ..' So she did, but not before asking a question, 'adopt a cowboy …that wouldn't be a line you're spinning me would it?' Gabe was still holding onto the woman he had fallen for and pulling back a little he smiled, removing his hat, 'Getting to know you better is what I hope for ..do you think you might like that?' he answered, his eyes filled with longing and his powerful physique steady as a rock. With a pounding heart and trying to think of a playing hard to get answer, Seraphina was then kissed so exquisitely by Gabe, that all she managed was to whisper 'Yes … I'd like that..'

And so began the massive, deep, grown up, romance of Seraphina and Gabe. Destiny had finally pulled these two born-to-be soulmates together from oceans apart. A small miracle.

What followed for Seraphina that holiday amounted to the ultimate romance-starved woman's wish list. Riding all day in God's Country, a landscape made for horse-loving soul mates. The last frontier and the place where the last Commanche fought to the end. For a long time the waves of immigrants moving across America in the mid nineteenth century had hardly touched the Texas Hill Country and the Commanche had held their ground. Even today there is a real sense of stepping back in time. Little has really changed, and the rich city slickers who have discovered this beautiful place build homes sympathetic to the landscape, keeping the palpable feel of the Romantic Wild West. Indian arrowheads can be picked up from the parched ground without looking too hard, left strewn on land that was humming with Apache, and later Comanche, warriors and their wives, hunting and growing, harvesting and living off the land, mixed in with the odd bit of raiding and kidnapping of settlers. Immigrant children were a prized novelty catch for some Comanche and once kidnapped, seldom came back alive. Those who did were imprinted indelibly after so much intimate contact with their captors and returned to civilization changed, educated in the ways of the Indian and attached to them, unable to relate to their own families.

Seraphina and Gabe swam on horseback in the magnificent Guadalupe River, danced the two-step in quaint venues in the little town and made passionate love before each dawn in her little log cabin. Passion on the ground when they snatched a stolen moment, losing the others on their trail rides, and under the moonlight, a hundred bales high in the big quiet barn. Seraphina felt far, far away from Wales but time was running out, her holiday of a lifetime was bowling along too fast. Soon she would be back at the shop running the business which no longer felt part of her real life. Unbeknown to Gabe and Seraphina, the other guests at the ranch all knew about their illicit romance, as did Florence, Marvin and the hot-tub maintenance man. Their passionate desire for one another needed to be kept secret because Gabe would lose his job if he was found to be romancing a paying guest. The lovers thought they'd been discreet, which they had, but unfortunately a little love note to his sweetheart – just a simple heart with a kiss and their names on it – had been found under Seraphina's pillow when Florence had been doing the rooms. The cat was out of the bag. Seraphina tended to be last in for breakfast on the ranch, glowing and famished. 'Too much testosterone I guess' piped up a lady from Louisiana within earshot of Seraphina one morning.

Suspicious that something was up, Seraphina knew she had to mention to Gabe the possibility of them having been found out, mortified that he might lose his job. The Texan cowboy and the Welsh shop keeper, who had only just met, from entirely different worlds, looked deep into each other's eyes. There it was, the acknowledgement that Gabe, like Seraphina, was yearning inside, tired of a loveless life, a life without intimacy, one where the divine driving force of passion and companionship and real love was absent. The knowledge that they both felt this was a moment of pure hope for Seraphina. Her soul ignited at the prospect of sharing a life with her lovely cowboy. Pulling her gently to him and kissing her, Gabe said, 'Well, that just about does it I guess, you'll have to adopt me now … we'll buy a little ranch and…', she went on to finish his sentence '.. and I can reorganize everything back home in Wales and be back here by the Spring.' They hugged and kissed, then stood back from one another, smiling, and giving a high five before looking skyward and whispering, 'Yee Haa'.

The flight home from her holiday of a lifetime was wrenching agony, Seraphina cried all the way to London and with every tear came more certainty that she was right to want to change her life forever. 'I can't go on like this, living a life I'm fed up with, I'm in love with Gabe and there's an end to it.', she sobbed. Sitting on the plane, when she thought she couldn't withstand the pain of separation a moment longer, she went a degree further and remembered what it had been like that morning with him in her log cabin. The sound of jingle-bobs and heavy leather chaps being dropped to the floor had become her divine wake-up call. Gabe, not saying a word bent forward and kissed her nose, she stretched her head back as he moved to her throat. Standing, he pulled back the American quilt and she soaked up the sight of him, his hard work torso, and the scent of the man she loved. He enveloped her body just by looking and sensing. The intensity of that morning and the depth of their feelings was declared to one another as love. A last kiss remembered now.

Hindsight is futile, but a crystal ball .... now that would have been useful and Seraphina really could have done with one. The crystal ball would have shown her that almost a year to the day that she first set foot in Texas in December 1998, she would have gone round in a full circle and arrived back at the drawing board of her romantic destiny. But now she was at the beginning of the circle, a grown intelligent woman swept away on the magic carpet of two weeks of bliss. Seraphina dismantled her cosy Welsh life. She put a manager in to run her shop, rented out her lovely cottage and in a tipsy moment of longing for Gabe and his lifestyle, went online and bought an open plane ticket back to Texas. Mum and Dad muttered a few words of caution, and friends warned her of the perils of believing in a holiday romance, but Seph would hear none of it. Gabe loved her and trusted her love for him, they had ultimately adopted one another. They gave their all, sharing common ground and companionship as well as deep love, so she was right to throw caution to the wind and in April 1999 she followed her heart back to Texas.

****

Racing through Passport Control and out into the bustling lobby of San Antonio Airport, she scanned the faces, searching for her love, yearning for his touch, when a strong, warm, tanned hand slipped round her waist from behind. Gabe had his woman back at last and, gently turning her to face him, he kissed her with such tenderness. Being reunited that beautiful sunny Spring day was the happiest moment of both their lives. They knew where they were going and had talked endlessly about their planned adventure on transatlantic phone calls. Walking out of the airport with Gabe at her side, Seraphina knew that her exquisite Odyssey had begun. There in the sunlit car park was Gabe's truck, towing a trailer with two horses on board. Within a few dreamy hours, the lovers were camped in the Texas Hill Country, making love under the bluest sky imaginable on a carpet of spring flowers. The months that followed were all that Seraphina had dreamed of and she and Gabe lived and loved outdoors, in that magic landscape which had the power to uplift the human spirit.

Chapter Four

Three months had passed since Seraphina had lost Gabe, her lover, her friend, her rock. There had been no goodbyes, instead a brick wall ending to their passionate affair, their Hill Country odyssey, and longed for marriage. Marooned now, back in her little shop in Wales, she had spent the New Millennium Eve alone, not a kiss or a firework came her way that night. Seraphina was heartbroken, as only a woman in her early thirties can be. All consuming grieving and shuddering tears poured out of the floodgates of her soul. All the bravado of following her heart crumpled in on Seraphina that dreadful day.... At Christmas she had flown back to Wales to tell her Mum and Dad the wonderful news that Gabe had proposed to her and that they were to be married the following Spring. Seraphina had come home to sell her cottage and her painted furniture business, she and Gabe were going to buy their dream ranch at last. Mum and Dad were so happy for her, they had never seen her look so glowing and alive. Back in Wales it had felt odd to Seraphina to be sleeping in a real bed and to enjoy a hot bath, after so many months of sleeping under the stars with Gabe and the horses. She'd stepped out that morning to do some last minute shopping before flying back to Texas, in time to

be reunited with Gabe for New Year's Eve, and had desperately tried to save a tiny fluttering bird with a broken leg stuck in the wing-mirror of her mother's car. The bird had been drawn by its own reflection and had trapped its foot in the metal rim encasing the mirror. Now frantic, it was unable to fly away from the grip round its now broken fragile leg. Seraphina cupped the little bird in her hand and tried and tried to wiggle the mirror to release the creature. Nothing worked, so she scrabbled in her handbag and found her nail scissors. She cupped the bird again, allowing it to become calm in her protective hand. Summoning all her courage, she had no choice but to snip through the tiny strand of skin still tethering the bird. Suddenly it flew off, she turned and watched it fly and wondered how it would survive and perch with only one leg. Would it topple every time and be doomed to a life of continual flight without respite? How would it forage? How would it sleep? A pre-emptive grief engulfed her, and she tried to calm her trembling hands. She walked back into the house to tell her Mum about the bird. Her mother was just putting the telephone down and scribbling a number on the notepad, looking terrible.
'What's up Mum? Hey that's a Texas phone number… what?' Taking her daughter's hand, Mum sat her down in Dad's armchair in the sitting room. 'Gabe's been killed – a road accident – his friend Chester the Gun has left his phone number – he needs you to call him.'

Without taking a breath, ghostly white, Seraphina went to the phone in the hall, 'There's been some mistake Mum, I'm sure of it.' Her hands were shaking and she just about managed to dial the number. Chester, Gabe's lifelong friend, answered her call, Seph knew him and could tell by his voice that the news was definitely bad. 'What's happened Chester … for Christ's sake .. what's happened?'
'Seraphina .. I'm so sorry .. I tried to save him .. we all tried .. Gabe's gone. We were in my pick-up on Highway 10, Gabe was driving when we got hit head on by a truck carrying logs .. the load had slipped … there were logs rolling everywhere …. There were two other fatalities and they had to close the road … there was so much wreckage … everywhere ..', Chester broke down on the phone and there was a long silence when the two of them just stayed on the line, trying to take it in. Chester went on, 'Seraphina there's something else you need to know ….Gabe bought you a wedding present, a gift and it's here for you.'
Seraphina was sobbing, 'Oh Chester … I just can't think right now .. send it to me …can you?'
Mum gave her distraught daughter a tissue and Chester continued, 'It's a little awkward to send …. Gabe bought you a ranch.' 'A ranch? .. Oh my God …..', Seraphina's Mum took the phone, her daughter was slumped on the hall carpet now, weeping. Chester explained that Probate could take a while and for Seph to sit tight in

Wales, until the lawyers appointed to look after Gabe's Estate got in touch.

Seraphina returned to her shop-life in Wales and licked her wounds. She held on to her cottage and pulled out of a deal to sell her business. Her survival instinct kicked in, she knew about the crippling effect of bereavement from past experience, when her lovely brother had died. Work had saved her then and she knew work would steady her now. She knew her job so well, she could keep going like a zombie if it came to that. For a while she steered clear of pink bubbly, her favourite drink, for fear she would tumble into a downward spiral and never recover. Mum and Dad stayed strong for their lovely daughter and prayed she'd recover from this unlucky romance. Willing herself with gritted teeth to survive Seraphina rose like tempered steel from the clinker of her broken heart. She kept going as if Gabe were only in the next room and not gone, or that he was simply outside gathering wood. Her emotions were dislocated from the fact, her subconscious mind knowing better than her that she simply wasn't ready to face life without her beloved cowboy at her side. After a while a fragile transposition evolved, she'd talked herself into believing that the romance with Gabe had been precious, a thing apart, but that her second love, was the Hill Country itself. It was that landscape, that special lifestyle which had moved her, gripped her, before she had even set eyes on Gabe. So she was protected from a spinstery life of bitterness and sad longing. Instead she was reconnected and spent hours on Ebay collecting and buying beautiful rare vintage cowboy-gear. Spurs, saddles, chaps, sleigh bells, Remington prints, wonderful rare books telling her more about her favourite place on earth. The great love of her life was still there for her, intact and seemingly loving her right back.

That day in her shop, the day the Deeds to her ranch had arrived in the post, three months after Gabe had been killed, business carried on as usual. Her old Dad came in to help out, like he always did, joking and keeping it light, which his daughter was grateful for. 'Well, well, well,' he said, 'Mum's given me the 'clecs So Gabe's ranch really has materialized .. well I'll be damned, and you've certainly got the right name for a lady rancher ..' Father and daughter chuckled as Dad did his impersonation of John Wayne.

It was no accident that she was named Seraphina Trinity Cody. It was in fact all planned that she should share a name with Col. William F. Cody, the legendary army scout, Indian fighter and buffalo hunter. Buffalo Bill Cody was regarded as a 'stupendous and inspiring' namesake by her paternal Welsh grandfather,

Jim, who was given the gift of naming his newborn granddaughter in the Spring of 1969.

On September 21st 1891 her grandfather had stood as a small boy of five in awe and trembling excitement on the platform of Cardiff railway station. The Welsh Capital let out a roar of cheers as the hefty steam-train tooted in to roost and spill its precious cargo into the heart of the Welsh Nation. Buffalo Bill And His Wild West Show had arrived, and what followed was reported as the most magical and exhilarating six days in the history of Wales. The man himself disembarked on horseback to a tumultuous clapping and 'The Greatest Showman On Earth leaned out of his saddle and plucked little Jim out of the dangerous crush with a God-like arm, to more loud cheers. Seraphina's grandfather had the experience of a lifetime. Firmly astride the Great Cowboy's horse and part of the Parade, he rode through the streets of Cardiff. Little Jim's elder brother, Idris, sworn on pain of death by their mother to 'Hold on tight to little Jim', anxiously called out, 'Don't worry, Jim! I'll see you at the end of the Parade .... I'm following behind,.. Whatever happens ... stay close to Buffalo Bill .. he'll look after you'
The crowd overwhelmed Idris as he surrendered to the spectacle of 'Savage' Indians riding bareback and whooping, while others beat strange drums and the original Deadwood Stage Coach nearly ran him over with its team of massive mules, adorned with lively Cowgirls

firing right into the air. Gun smoke and war-paint, horse-sweat and laughter, whips cracking and the deafening clatter of spark-flying steel-shod horse's hooves and the sight of an imperious young woman, a living legend, the crack shot Miss Annie Oakley who was today demurely hound-trotting, side-saddle on a 'light-as-a-fairy' bay mare. The people of Wales adored her and she had this to say about them:

'As for Cardiff, we are all delighted with it. The people here appear to be very intelligent – much more so than the people in the north of England – and their behaviour is wonderfully good. Another good reason for liking Cardiff is the business done – the best of all the towns.'

By the time Idris caught up with his little brother he was exhilarated and exhausted. He needn't have worried and upon enquiring at the new base-camp that was Buffalo Bill's domain, he was solicitously shown to a huge tent by a terrifying, friendly 'Red Indian' in full war-paint and a halo of feathers. Idris pulled back the heavy elk-hide door flap and was met with a scene he'd remember in manhood. A twinkling array of spurs and bridles with concho-bedecked cheek-pieces and silver bits. Buffalo-hide bedrolls and lines of embroidered cowboy boots and chaps with buckles and fringes. Squeals of laughter were coming from little Jim sitting on a huge pile of saddles and gunbelts, being tickled affectionately by two young crack-shot babysitters. 'Idris! Idris!' Jim shouted, 'You'll never believe what happened to me today!' They ran into each other's arms and laughed and laughed. Idris was sixteen and had never met such fascinating young ladies as Jim's real Cowgirl babysitters that memorable day. 'Howdy Idris, allow me to introduce ourselves, this here is Trinity and I'm Seraphina, Cardiff is a mighty fine city, I must say.' Idris blushed from his head to his toes, from his Welsh cloth cap to his hob-nailed boots.

So there it was, a collage of memories collated in a name, Seraphina Trinity Cody.

Chapter Five

On the threshold of a lady rancher's life, that stormy March day in her shop, Seph took a little deer-skin pouch off her key-ring, the treasured keepsake from her Hill Country romance. The small bouquet garni of juniper-ash or 'cedar' as it was commonly known, was cherished and from time to time she'd open the little homemade pouch and bury her nose inside to inhale deeply. Seraphina let the scent work its magic that day, the shop bell jingling with customers coming and going, Dad still amusing himself with his cowboy impersonations and Mum taking a closer look at the map which had come with the Deeds. 'Gosh, the little ranch looks pretty remote ..' quavered Mum, prompting Seraphina to remember, to drift back. Although she'd never seen the ranch, she knew the landscape it was a part of. Not even the heavy smell of solvent-based paints and varnish in her shop could mask the intense perfume emanating from the small pouch, the absolute signature-scent of The Texas Hill Country. The ubiquitous juniper-ash shrub had self-seeded everywhere and taken the place of the lush grassland which had been chewed to nothing by half a century of over-grazing, long after the last remaining wild Native Indian was swept away. The scent of the Texas Hill Country ..... slightly medicinal, a super-clean super-fresh invigorating smell that, once absorbed and inhaled, leaves behind a heady, lingering, soft musky sensation and for Seraphina, it was unforgettable and intensely evocative. She remembered those halcyon days with such deep emotion, when she was in love and loved, glowing, tanned, alive.

Out in the Hills with Gabe, she was wearing a pair of rare 19th Century ladies' spurs with love-heart 'buttons' and tiny spinning stars, set in hand-made steel shanks, her feet clad in knee-high mule skin cowboy boots, embroidered and stack-heeled. Her blue denim Wranglers overlaid with a pair of Gabe's custom-made chaps in soft brown leather, a fringe of contrasting cream, running vertically from hip to heel. On the outside of each thigh, hand-tooled leather pockets were stitched with matching fringe round the edges.

The conchos decorating the latigo leg-fastenings, were old Mexican coins, converted with welded loops. Her belt buckle glinted in the white clean sunlight and showed an engraved galloping horse, on pure silver. The vintage deer skin shirt she wore was finely fringed and embroidered with tiny flowers in blue and orange thread. Her wrists were protected by 'cuffs', authentic, hand-tooled, her fingers free. The hat she wore was a shallow-crown Stetson, the wide almost horizontal brim, decked with a garland of fresh wild flowers. She'd picked brilliant red 'Mexican Paintbrushes', fiery 'Indian Blankets' and a gorgeous Texas Big Bend Bluebonnet and had linked them daisy-chain style. A red cotton handkerchief was tied round her neck. Red, her horse, grazed nearby, a liver-chestnut gelding, a pure-bred American Quarter Horse of the old type, smaller and leaner than today's evolved stock and a perfect match for Seraphina. What a sight they made, standing on top of the bluff, the little horse, head up, ears pricked forward and nostrils flared, while sensing his surroundings and contemplating territory instinctively. He was bedecked with a vintage Western saddle over a red fringed blanket. The deep, dark, shiny leather, set-off spectacularly by the bright crimson. The saddle was a work of art, yet well used and worthy, with hand-tooled brimful floral hearts on the cantle, the fenders, the skirt. The saddle horn was made for work and the maker had left nothing to chance, using the traditional method to keep the wear and tear of 'roping' at bay – the skin of a goat's scrotum, applied like cling film, yet tough as old boots, added a final touch of workish glory. The bridle was bitless and minimalist, the maximum any self-respecting Quarter horse needed. The breast-plate centered on another brimful floral heart, cut out this time, silhouetted against the animal's deep chest. Gabe had gone to gather wood so Seraphina hopped back in the saddle that glorious Spring day and trotted off round the bluff, down a steep incline, zig-zagging to the edge of Turtle Creek. Named so because fresh-water turtles bobbed merrily about in it. As she sat still at the water's edge, sure enough, every-so-often, a gorgeous, perky little turtle would clamber out of the water and have a short sunbathe on the warm rocky creek bank. Each turtle coloured fantastically, in bright, bright greens and yellows, in modernistic markings as if they knew the New Millennium was approaching. That they were absolutely of the 21st Century and not some throw-back from pre-ice-age times. The sight of them, busy and lively, paddling away in the clear water on the crest of a mini wave, was heartwarming. The whole world it seemed, was getting 'spified-up' and sparkly, at the realization that a brand-spanking new century was dawning. If ever a landscape had been designed to soothe the soul, then this Hill Country was it. Small unchallenging hills with water winding its way round and about, quenching the thirst of the prolific wildlife. Deer and more deer, feral hogs and designer piglets, armadillos ..... fabulous prehistoric, invincible armadillos. Spring really was bursting out all over. Carpet upon carpet of flowers, red, orange, blue and purple, rolled out like shaggy rugs, glowing on saffron parched earth. The glint of white-grey exposed rock ledges, punctuated the ground – a psychedelic seabed, which is precisely what the land had been, a zillion million years before. Seraphina was scuba-diving now, on horse-back, breathing scented oxygen.

'Come on then' her Welsh Mum scolded, tapping her watch, impatient, 'It's one o'clock, they'll all be awake now in Texas'
It was time for Seraphina to call the Probate lawyers, acknowledge Gabe's gift and change her life – again.
'Right then Mum, let's get a pen and paper ready and call 'em up.'

Chapter Six

Seraphina dialled the number in Texas...
Meanwhile her father was under strict instructions to 'front' the shop and deal with the

customers, so she could be left uninterrupted on the phone in the workshop, with her mother keeping a vigil. Seraphina cleared her throat and took a deep breath...'Good Morning, I'd like to speak to whoever is dealing with The Turtle Creek Estate. It's Miss Cody, calling from Wales in the UK ... I see ... yes ... I'm so sorry ... Goodbye.' The colour drained from her mother's face as she clutched her daughter's arm. 'It's ok Mum, calm down, I dialled the wrong number, that's all. Anyway, one thing's for certain, that Walmart in 'them there hills', sure is friendly.' Smiling, Seraphina dialled again. 'Good morning, I'd like to speak to whoever is dealing with The Turtle Creek Estate. It's Miss Cody calling from Wales in the UK .... I see.... yes .... umm.. ok .... good heavens .... really ..... I see ...... yes .... umm ..... ok .... go on .... right .... yes ....yus .... yup ..... nope .... yup ..' The one-sided conversation drove her Welsh mother mad. She was desperate for the 'clecs' the nitty-gritty detail. Her only clues were coming from the rapid, cryptic notes Seraphina was dashing down on the thick white notepad. Mum and Dad, together now, were both straining over their daughter's shoulder reading her scribbles … 'Edwards Aquifer …. Water …… borehole …dynamite …… cracked founds … illegal elex …. tapped … mighty dangerous .. roundin'up req … creek fouled up .. dead bovine … access … dirt track … flooded …nearly blind goat ..gun.'

Seraphina kept scribbling away on the notepad and 'yupping' a lot. Her parents were reading her notes out loud, as if trying them in different tones and facial expressions would somehow expand their meaning.
'A gun? What would she want with a gun?' Mum over-emphasized. 'To shoot the goat, I shouldn't wonder,' said Dad. 'Don't be ridiculous, they have vets in Texas, don't they?'
'Well yes, she'll need the gun to give the vet, so he can shoot the goat.' said Dad. Seraphina glared at her parents to be quiet, and took charge of her monosyllabic conversation, with her best Welsh 'blag' tone, wingin' and prayin' it.
'Right then Mr Peterson, you've given me an excellent run-down on the state of my Estate, for which I'm extremely grateful. I'd like you to Fed Ex the legal documents for signing and I will spend the rest of today digesting all the information you have kindly given me. Tomorrow I will telephone again, with answers to the more pressing decisions you require. In the meantime, please thank my new neighbour Eve Buchanan for looking after the horses over at her place and explain that I will square-up as soon as I get there.'
Mr Peterson interrupted his fascinating new Welsh client. 'You mean you actually plan to live on the ranch?'
'Well of course I do Mr Peterson, it's the opportunity of a life-time isn't it?'.... 'If you say so, Mam.'

She rounded off the conversation,…'Now, it will take me the best part of a month to put my affairs in order, here in Wales. Today is March 31st, so shall we say I'll be arriving in Texas May 1st, or thereabouts?'

'Yes Mam.' Seph put the phone down.

Her expression was pensive that afternoon, all afternoon in fact. She'd been left alone in her busy workshop with all the work to be done. Mum and Dad sent home, to mull over the adventure that lay ahead for their daughter. Sanding and scraping and painting and gilding and dealing with the customers, went on as usual that day. Except every-so-often a bubbling-up of excitement welled up inside her. She had a lot to do and a month to do it in.

Money, she was going to need money to run Turtle Creek Ranch and raising it was her first priority. So popular was her little going concern, her painted furniture shop, that by tea-time she had sold the business. A couple who'd been interested before, were delighted when they got the call from Seraphina late that afternoon. They were prepared to close the deal within four weeks, provided she started showing them the ropes immediately and provided Seraphina made herself available, by telephone in Texas, to troubleshoot when required. Next she called her friend Lewis, who had a buyer for her cottage within days. The pot was filling up, as she cobbled together a guessed cashflow forecast with an optimistic bias and a glorious heading : Year One At Turtle Creek.

Sitting alone at home that evening, she switched on her 'bucking-horse' lamp and switched off her mind for an hour or so, quietly sipping a glass of wine and enjoying the lovely interior she had created in her Welsh cottage. Every curtain wore a vintage spur tie-back and the throw on her sofa was a white-tail deer hide. An old pair of chaps hung on the wall, like a museum exhibit. Antlers were her coat-hooks and sleigh bells the light-pull. Stetsons and Homburgs and a 'carpet-bag' Sears & Roebuck side-saddle decorated one corner. Loads of lovely signed First Editions filled another corner. Her favourite artist's work hung on the walls, 'Six Pack Saturday Night' and 'Sharing An Apple', both by Tom Ryan, one of the great Cowboy Artists Of America. An old Welsh lectern cradled a just-in-time photographic record, The North American Indian – The Complete Portfolios – by Edward S. Curtis. The swatch of fabric placemats on her coffee-come-supper table, were decorated with different coloured cowboy boots, in a row. Even the cruet was linked, a pair of hand-painted cacti, one for salt, one for pepper. The telephone rang, it was her friend Rosey, calling from the local library. 'Hi Seph, I've managed to get those books you asked for, I'm on my way home, so I'll drop them round if you like.' 'Thanks that would be great, there's a bottle of wine open, if you fancy a glass.' She told Rosey the news and a promise

was made, that she'd 'be out for a visit, by hook or by crook.'
Later that evening, after a long hot bath, Seraphina got an early night and fell asleep with the pile of library books on top of her, still open, on her bed. They were sensible subject matter for a first-time lady rancher and included Goat Husbandry, Self Sufficiency, How To Handle A Mule, and Boreholes – A Civil Engineers Guide.

Next day it was all systems go, Seraphina making a dawn-breaking start at the shop. The 'To Do' lists, still plastered all over the walls, had risen from 1-37 to 1-49. A mountain of old French furniture needed painting, restoring, gilding, waxing, gluing, clamping, customizing, finishing, delivering. She slogged non-stop, all day and had reduced the daunting lists quite a bit by seven that evening.
Next day she repeated the whole exercise again, only this time teaching the soon-to-be new Proprietors how to do everything as she went along. Trying to condense twenty years of experience and skill, determinedly understating how difficult the job was.
With all that was tumbling in, she had still managed to produce a coherent, she thought, list of suitable answers for the Probate lawyer in Texas, regarding the pressing matters of her newly acquired Turtle Creek Ranch.

Chapter Seven

Seraphina was so busy organizing everything before heading West for her new life, that the days and weeks flew by. Her shop was a hive of activity, the nearest a honed skill gets to mass-production. Intense days of express-gilding and hand-painting, the timely task of French Polishing carried out at ninety miles an hour. At the end of each back-breaking day, Seraphina locked the doors and turned the window sign to Closed and put on her favorite CD at a lilting blast. 'Steve Earle and The Del McCoury Band', described by Seraphina as, 'A sort of olde pioneery fiddling sound portrayed by Mozart' Gabe had taken her to see the band perform live in Bandera, Texas and she had the happiest memory of them dancing the night away.

Burning the midnight oil, reading everything she could on the survival skills she would need for where she was going, alone, had kept her mind off grieving for Gabe. If she never read another book on Goat Husbandry, Self Sufficiency, How To Handle A Mule, and Boreholes – A Civil Engineers' Guide, it would be a day too soon.

She was really excited now, about what lay ahead, all the things she loved about where she was going, were about to become a reality again. She knew the joy of striding out on an early Texas Winter morning, with a pair of dogs and a good gun. It was Gabe who had taught her to shoot. Her morning constitutional back then, included firing a hundred rounds from a borrowed gun at inanimate targets, the gun-fire was deafening and made the natural sounds seem all the more pacifying and glorious when she stopped. Bird song and mildly creaking branches, buzzing insects and snuffling armadillos. Pink butterflies, unperturbed by the acrid smell of gun smoke, swirled around the trunk of a huge gnarled oak tree, which creaked and swayed over round, stumpy cacti. The rock they appeared to be growing out of was patterned with sea-shell fossils and a million pretty shapes, on the ancient seabed that was The Texas Hill Country. Seraphina was looking forward to the wonderful warm sunshine of Texas, away from the cold Welsh rain. The heat, 110 degrees centigrade in the shade in Summer, would send her and Gabe to take cool refuge at Lake Buchanan, hauling the trailer with the horses on board, Lightning and little Red. They'd camp on the shore of the huge freshwater lake, like a small ocean. Clear blue sky, deep clear water, filled with swimming turtles and big fish. It was the time of the Full Moon, so they'd ride at night when it was cooler. Glorious days were spent swimming in the lake with the horses alongside on lead reins, submerged and splashing in the divine chilled water. The horses with their shining, glinting, soaked coats dried off in the dazzling sun, and Gabe and Seraphina

would take another swim, just the two of them, far out in the heavenly lake. Nudged and tapped by nosy turtles. The evenings were lit up with the awesome, massive, touchable, round full moon, described by early settlers as a Comanche Moon, a thing to fear with all your heart as you quivered behind a wood door waiting to be scalped. They'd saddle up and ride out, both looking amazing. Healthy, tanned and shiny, wearing gorgeous chaps and vintage spurs, cowboy hats and conker leather heavy gunbelts, loaded with loaded pistols.
Seraphina astride Red posed for Gabe to take a photo., and her expression was pure happiness. The two modern cowboys had the time of their lives on those moonlit rides. There was nothing smaltzy about them, the outings were pure hilarious adventure. Mounted shooting was on the menu, which entailed galloping at full pelt and shooting at targets. The first night before firing the first loud shot, neither of them knew how the horses would react. 'Well there's only one way to find out!' shouted Gabe over the sound of galloping hooves, 'On the count of three then!' screamed Seraphina, 'One!Two!Three!' The sound cracked out, both horses bucking like hell and the riders weak with laughter, dumped on the ground with smoking guns.

‘Come on Dad, that’s enough reminiscing, onward and upward ..’ They were packing the last of her personal belongings from the shop in preparation for handing over the keys to the new owners.
‘I can’t believe we nearly forgot that..’, Seraphina reached up to take the picture down then changed her mind and stood back to look again before wrapping it to take to Texas with her. The portrait of William F. Cody was a gift from her paternal grandfather and her namesake. She’d grown up with the likeness of this interesting famous man hanging on her bedroom wall since she was old enough to remember and it showed him wearing fringed buckskins, his face looked out charismatically from under his wide brimmed hat. A groomed silken moustache complemented his golden locks. The painting showed him in his younger prime, before he was known as Buffalo Bill and touring the world with his Wild West Show. The long scar on one side of his face was illustrated too but it in no way detracted from his astonishing presence and her grandfather had glued a description of Cody cut out from an old newspaper and pasted it on the back of his gift to Seraphina. They were the words of Major Burke, a longtime friend and promoter of Bill reflecting on their first accidental meeting, and he was greatly impressed, later recalling ‘I had met a god … in my life. I came upon him just at sunset one night, out on the Missouri, and the reflection of the light from the river was shining up straight

into his face and lighting it up like some kind of an aura. He was on horseback, and I thought then that he was the handsomest, straightest, finest man that I had ever seen in my life. I still think so' Carefully lifting her painting from the old hook on the shop wall Seph sighed knowing the imprint of her grandfather's love for such things, this short period in American history, had shaped her life, inspired her and brought her to where she was right now – heading off into the sunset where the last Comanche had thrived. She pulled herself together, gingerly sellotaping the bubble-wrap around what felt to her, at that moment, like a palpable pulsing energy, emanating from this treasured picture. '.. right focus … focus on the present .. come on girl', she whispered to herself before looking up with a bright smile to greet the new owners of her shop and business. They were a great couple and Seraphina was confident that they would make a go of it. She'd trained them well and they'd driven a hard bargain, but she didn't mind, nothing was going to stop her selling up and moving to the ranch. But she had one last thing to do, a final solo buying trip to France, to buy stock for the shop. It had been promised to the new owners and was part of the deal. Seraphina's expertise in buying old and antique French furniture was honed. She could walk down row upon row of French fruitwood armoires and know in a heartbeat, the ones worth buying, no matter how persuasive the French dealers were, in their barns full to the rafters. Keeping it short as she surveyed each piece, 'non ..non... Oui....non.....non..non', and so on, before handing over a wad of cash. She was not looking forward to this last French trip, it was a lonely business and there'd be too much time to dwell on Gabe's death. After a long drive from home, she set off from Portsmouth on the ferry in a seven and a half ton cargo truck. It was noisy and dirty and the cab smelled of other people's hamburgers. It was a hire vehicle, so the radio didn't work and the ashtray was missing. An unticking clock gave the wrong time. She had three hundred miles to drive and hours to take in the fact that she was running to Gabe in The Hill Country and he wouldn't be there. She would be living and loving him in the empty space he'd left behind. She would be alone in the yearned-for landscape that she held so dear, and now she quaked more than a little at the boldness of her move to Texas.

The dealers in France all knew Seraphina, so in that sense the exercise was pretty painless. The familiar destination reached and the buying done, she headed back to Wales with blistered fingers from all the painting, and stiff tendons in her wrists from the days of lifting and shoving solid lumps of French furniture onto and into the truck. The ferry was getting ready to sail back to England. 'Phew ... am I glad that's over.' She breathed a sigh of relief and grabbed her mobile phone.'Yoo Hoo .. Hi Mum, how's it going?' Her mother was glad to hear her voice and immediately asked if she had eaten, she hadn't, although she loved eating and was a great cook but somehow she always managed to forget and only remembered when she started feeling faint. Then she would order steak and chips with all the trimmings. 'How's Max?'

'He's fine darling', her mother reassured her. 'He's had a good supper and is fast asleep on your father's lap.' This sent Seraphina into peals of laughter because Max, her beloved dog, was a Gordon Setter, the size of a small pony, and he only climbed onto other people's laps when he was missing his mistress. 'I'll be home around 4 am .. don't worry, I'm going to take a nap after my steak and chips.'

'We're dying to see you, your father and I were just saying how brave you are and how proud of you we are. Now go and get a hot meal, put your feet up for a few hours and drive carefully.'

'Ok, love to you all and give Max a big squash from me. Oh and by the way, I've bought some fab pieces for the shop. Bye then, bye.'

The huge hydraulics started winding up the steel embarkation ramps of the ship, Seraphina stuffed her phone in her pocket and jumped out of the freezing cab, locked all the doors and bolted a hefty padlock on the steel roller-shutter at the rear of the truck. She checked the undercarriage with the torch her mother had given her for Christmas. 'Ok, no suspicious packages anywhere, I'll just check the front wheel axles.' She was lying on the deck now, not bothered about the pools of diesel, she was dressed for it. 501 Levi's, Caterpillar steel toe-capped boots and a battered, thick brown leather jacket. She knew her truck would be checked by sniffer dogs and that sometimes other people's people or drugs could be strapped to an unsuspecting wagon, just to get them through customs and on to British soil. She was vulnerable because she was a woman, alone. 'Right, find the Ladies and pee, for pity's sake.' She began the long climb from the bowels of the ship, up seven flights of steep, steel stairways. Fighting claustrophobia, she gasped, her legs turned to jelly. So many hours driving, after a day of loading the truck and using every ounce of strength to do it, had just about finished Seraphina off. She faltered for a split second, knelt and wept from exhaustion.

Chapter Eight

It was April 30th 2000, she'd celebrated her thirty-first birthday that month and the day for departure had finally arrived, she was flying to San Antonio from where she'd drive on to her sight unseen Texas ranch. Seraphina was wearing her favourite collected vintage cowboy gear, chaps, spurs, hat, the whole deal, so an authentically dressed new lady ranch owner bestowed on her friends an intriguing picture as she said her farewells. She took one final stroll around her now empty cottage before she closed the front door behind her and walked the short distance to the graveside of her beloved brother who had died tragically, aged twenty-six when Seph was just twenty-one. Taking a calming deep breath as she placed a sprig of Mimosa at the base of the simple headstone, 'Hey Tim .. if there is a Heaven and you're in it, find Gabe, shake his hand and get to know eachother, the idea of that happening brings me such comfort my lovely, dear brother … I miss you.' She turned and headed up the High Street of the small Welsh market town she'd called home since she was sixteen.

'Hey Seph! Don't squat in your spurs!', called out a local young lad. 'Not a chance, dopey!' she called back.

'I'm coming to visit mind, by hook or by crook', reminded Rosey.

'Lookin' forward to it', drawled Seraphina for a joke.

'Don't forget us now Cariad!', shouted Morgan as he whizzed past on his police bicycle. Conjuring up her best John Wayne impersonation she answered, 'That'll be the day.' The shopkeepers were coming out of their individual emporia to stand on the step and wave and ooh and ahh, at the sight of Seraphina actually wearing something that wasn't covered in paint. A big yellow Welsh daffodil was slipped into her cowboy hatband by her friend Juliette, as she passed her little florist shop. 'Juliette I'll be waiting for you to visit, don't forget mind', Seraphina said.

She was coming to the Town Hall Monument, winding her way to her parent's home for her taxi to the airport. She stood and read the names of all the local lovely Welsh boys, all that remained of them now carved in stone, lost forever in two World Wars. She hadn't noticed that you could hear a pin drop and as she turned to take one more look down the High Street of her small Welsh world, she found that a few of the boys from the local Male Voice Choir had stealthily assembled to quietly hum their rendition of the famous Welsh song 'We'll Keep A Welcome In The Hillside.' Neil and Cath were there, they'd driven all the way down from the Welsh Valleys to wish her luck and to give her the prettiest little chiming French clock, she'd ever seen, 'To put on the mantel of that log cabin of yours' rasped Neil. Seraphina hadn't known she was loved, and was touched so deeply, her vintage spurs with the love-heart buttons trembled, and her face was ashen, time stood still for too many heartbeats. When she finally got to her parent's house, she was late and Mum and Dad had already organized her bags in a neat row outside the door, ready for the taxi. Max leapt up at her, licking her face and wagging his tail. His huge front paws resting on her shoulders as he looked her square in the face with his big brown eyes. It is at times like this that a whirl of painful feelings can creep up on you and get you by the throat unawares, squeezing, squeezing. This was one of those times. Max her beloved dog and faithful friend, had been usurped by Gabe's legacy. Her dog was bewildered and put out by all the packing and upheaval, upset at finding himself sharing a bed with Seraphina's mother's yapping Yorkshire Terrier, in a different house without his mistress. The taxi was waiting, the bags were on board. Seraphina could not leave him. She just could not leave Max behind. With a melon-size lump in her throat, she did. With tears pouring down their cheeks, Mum and Dad and their treasured daughter hugged and said Goodbye. 'See you in a few months, Mum .. see you before Christmas, Dad' She chinked into the waiting taxi, catching her spurs as she pulled the door shut and just sat like a zombie, as she said goodbye to Wales, and everything she knew.

****

With burning rubber, the plane screeched onto the runway at San Antonio airport. Seraphina hit the ground unsteady, but determined. Standing at the Hertz Hire Car desk she thought aloud ... 'No more bigsadgoodbyeitis!', the man behind the desk smiled and handed her the car keys.

Seraphina was finally on her way to Droversville, and the dog-eared copy of A Cowboy At Work was by her side on the passenger seat. Tangled round the steering wheel was a map, which she'd done her best to memorize on the long flight over. It was getting dark and she checked into a motel by around ten that night, the arrangement being to collect final directions from the Probate lawyers' office on the following morning. It had been four months since she'd last been in Droversville and land prices were going through the roof. She remembered before she left that the talk was about big residential development and all the stuff that comes when a gorgeous spot gets spotted. It seemed a long way off back then, when you could buy a chunk of Hill Country for a few hundred dollars an acre. Wealthy business people were setting up home left, right and centre, in a well-publicized, safe, healthy environment. Boreholes were drying up as the first level of aquifer was sucked dry. Everyone started blowing up rock with dynamite, to go deeper to the second aquifer and suck that dry too, affecting an entire eco-system, some thought. Reservoirs were built, more planned and fought over. Huge contracts and dollars at stake, unresolved for the time being. Gated Communities were all the rage, tracts of land carved up, built on, and fenced in with guards and walkie-talkies at the entrance, in case a squirrel had the temerity to enquire after its favourite nut tree. City Slickers were flocking in, 'working from home' with giant satellite dishes screwed onto pretend-shingle rooftops. Shopping Malls were springing up, very smart restaurants were upstaging favourite watering and eating holes. Traffic was building up and even 'rush-hours' evolved. Walmart had never done so well before in this out-of-the-way town.

New Car salesmen set up showrooms of shiny 'runarounds', instead of cowboy trucks and trailers. Even the saddle shops were selling pink sequined saddle blankets and Ginseng for horses. Every builder, carpenter, plumber, electrician, brick-layer and surveyor was working flat out seven days a week including Thanksgiving, their four-legged friends left grazing and unridden.

That sunny May morning, when Seraphina finally got to set eyes on Turtle Creek Ranch, she had driven into town on a route she remembered. The difference this time was hard to believe. As she looked up at the familiar landscape of rugged hills skirting the town, they were dotted with countless properties, mansions in various stages of being built, cranes and cement mixers and a Real Estate sign saying 'Welcome to Hillywood' stood out like a beacon. She parked up outside the Probate lawyer's office and took a deep breath before walking in. It took a while before Seraphina got out of the habit of wearing chaps and spurs for everything, including grocery shopping and coffee mornings. So when she walked into the office in town to collect her ranch, she cut quite a dash. It amused Mr Peterson and Mr Sydney and the two long-legged nyloned secretaries and the other clients in the waiting room. Seraphina jingle-bobbed her way round the office and was invited to take a seat, half an hour later, she sauntered out with a handwritten map, one door key and a sheaf of utility bumph to get on with. Mr Peterson also handed her the bill 'so far'...$1100.00 for the removal of Cricket the goat's eyeball and the dehorning required to stop the horns in-growing again and possibly taking out the other eye. $800.00 for the removal of the dead cow that was poisoning the creek and water supply. $500.00 to pick up Betsy and Leopold, the two mules who had run amok all the way to Medina and had holed up with a dainty Peruvian Gaited pony, who was eternally grateful that Leopold was a mutant and therefore sterile, there would be no mulettes with a gait to die for. $1600.00 for the damage done by Betsy and Leopold to the trailer they were brought home in. The cherry on the cake of her sweet inheritance, that day, was a bill for $3000.00 from McDonald's for damage done 'everywhere really', when Dozer the longhorn bull, who wasn't even on Seraphina's chattel list, lured presumably, by the bright lights of 'Hillywood', led her newly acquired herd of mooing babes into the hamburger joint for breakfast. 'I see, well, good heavens' said Seraphina, as she prized a thick wad of $100 bills from inside her waistband. She counted out $7000.00 and asked for a receipt. Mr. Peterson gave her a tin of sweets with a bucking horse on the lid.

Chapter Nine

When deciding where to live in this magical part of the world an important question needed to be asked : 'Restricted' or 'Unrestricted', that was the conundrum on some people's lips. It was the difference between 'people of the land', who believed they were the 'caretakers', not owners, even though they actually owned a portion of 'God's Country', versus outsiders, who bought the God-given spread and owned it to fence it in and possess it wholeheartedly. The old-timers and their spunky offspring had a liberty bestowed upon them, which they didn't recognize back then. It came from the fact they were born in a place where not many people wanted to live. In those days, the developers didn't care enough to make rules and keep up appearances by making 'restrictions' on the land. That had changed now and the world and his wife wanted a piece of The Texas Hill Country. So there were provisos: 'Restrictions', which meant a standard was formulated. Sometimes the minimum size house-build allowed was 3000 square feet and most went for bigger options. So no matter how rich you were, if you bought 'Restricted' land and all you wanted to build was a little log cabin, then you had to order a pretend one and have it built in the back yard of the rather lovely, architect designed, sprawling mansion called home, as a quaint extra, along with the carpets and curtains. If you lived on 'Unrestricted' land you could pee on your own tree and build anything you could.

Some parked a trailer and lived in that and didn't bother building a house. Others lived in a beautiful authentic log cabin or timber-framed house with flowers and horses and super-duper neighbours and a burbling creek that the outsiders were deprived of. 'Live' water was the ultimate trophy and didn't come cheap. One enterprising young man from Dallas understood there was extra money to be made with 'Live', free-flowing gushing spring water. He managed to find the only bit of Texas Hill Country that was unwanted and dirt cheap, on the edge of a busy highway, with one pimply hill. He speculated with a million tons of concrete and pumps and, like God himself, created, 'Live' water. Carved up and fenced in, the 'Restricted Gated Community', sold its Hill Country Homes like hot cakes and if you wanted to live on the head of the pimple itself, it cost more. The fantastic glossy brochure, portrayed the contrived live watery world, as exquisite. So the place was in transition but only on the surface. The Hill Country itself had its own plans and could withstand a plethora of hard working, well educated, shiny natives. The indigenous Native American Indians fed and housed themselves for centuries on the very spot supposedly untouched and just rediscovered. There was plenty to go round and besides it was kick-starting the local economy, big time. Disaffected cowboys and cowgirls were getting interested again, earning dollars and taking a new direction. Jaded small ranch owners were selling up and living differently, with a lifetime of good memories to fall back on. All of them richer and some happier. The Texas Hill Country was like a beautiful natural woman, being taken aside like a lily and gilded just a little. Seraphina didn't care if someone lived in a mansion or a trailer, all she cared about was how they were as human beings. She had worked out by now, that 'Most people were nice and if you didn't like someone, it was just because you didn't really know them.' Optimism had always been her soulmate.

The sun was shining and Seraphina was almost at her sight-unseen, gift of a ranch. Hungry and excited and a lot slimmer since debulking her waistband of $7000.00, she couldn't resist pulling over at the McDonald's that her livestock had purportedly stampeded through, to pick up brunch. There were workmen all over the place hammering and cementing and sweeping up shards of broken glass and half eaten hamburgers. A pink kitten-heel lady's shoe was being touted at the counter as lost property. Two glamorous Dallas ladies were waiting for their Big Macs, annoyed at the unusually slow service.
'Those awful hilly-billy unrestricted people with their hilly-billy cows.'
'Round 'em up and kick 'em out, that's what I say.'

Clutching the wobbly hand-drawn map, Seraphina drove on through town a little and pulled up overlooking the Guadalupe River. Tucking in to her $3000.00 McDonald's brunch, she gazed down at the river and the exact spot where she and Gabe used to swim with the horses.

She remembered how they would ride down from the hills, right through Droversville and stop at the Bank for Seraphina to lean out of the saddle and use the cash machine. Stocking up on small supplies, just for the fun of going through town, shopping on horseback, chatting to anyone who wound down a car window to say Howdy. Often, they would snatch a cheap meal, with Lightning and Red tied up to a tree in the busy car park, enjoying all the fuss being made of them by the kids. Gabe giving Seraphina a leg-up back into the saddle, with a soft squeeze would say 'Ok boys, bath time', and they'd ride on down under the bridge and take the horses in the beautiful Guadalupe River.

Drying off in the sun, they would lay down on the grassy riverbank and 'get the map out'. She'd hand Gabe a pen and he'd draw all the trails they had ridden over the weeks, on top of the printed routes. They had been all over the place and it always amazed Seraphina how far and wide they had travelled together, on those joyous trips with the horses. Before heading back to the hills, they'd ride over to a local bar where Gabe was known and they'd share a pitcher of iced tea with lemons floating in it, cool and refreshing and something Seraphina found delicious and new. The intensity of their romance was clearly visible to those they met and people would smile and twinkle around them. The warmth of their friendship and glow of their feelings for one another was pretty to see, one lady commenting 'Ain't you pair cute.'

'Wow! Can't believe I'm back!' Seraphina said out loud to herself, sounding hollow, gingerly munching away, almost choking on her emotion, knowing Gabe was gone, knowing she would never touch him again, or feel the warmth of his hand round her waist, or the scent of his body close to hers. A terrible gut-wrenching sadness stopped her from eating and she changed her mind about going straight to the ranch and drove over to Walmart to stock up instead. She had a feeling that she was going to need more than a bag of groceries. Two full shopping trolleys later, she was back at the car loading the trunk, ready for the off. Kerosene lamps, sleeping bag, gallons of bottled water, a picnic set, camping cooker, pots and pans, pillows, blankets, cowboy coffee-pot, matches, lighter fuel, firelighters, toilet tissue, bath towels, soap, shampoo, washing detergent, toilet cleaner, multi-surface cleaner, window cleaner, a copy of American Vogue, a local newspaper and a fishing rod. The only things she didn't have that day, were the only two things Gabe said you actually needed in the Hill Country, 'An axe and a rifle'. The Hertz

hire car was bursting with supplies and suitcases and maps. Seraphina had hired it for the week, to give her time to get used to driving Gabe's open pick-up which was waiting for her at the ranch.
Coming off the Highway, she started the winding drive to her longed for life. She took a deep breath and opened the window, feeling tense and sick, the realization that she would be sleeping alone in the middle of nowhere had crept up on her and was squeezing her by the throat.
Unbeknown to Seraphina there was a little more to the ranch, than she knew at that moment, it was partly to do with the log cabin. This wasn't just any old cabin, it had been custom built for her by Gabe.
Aged seventeen Gabe had made a down payment on the 350 acres of land at Turtle Creek and twenty-five years later he'd finished paying for it, aged forty-two. He'd proposed to Seraphina on his forty second birthday, knowing that if she said yes, he was going to surprise her with the little ranch, it was going to be his wedding present to her. Seraphina gave him the answer he hoped for, standing on a ridge overlooking Droversville, as the sun rose that wonderful morning. Unbeknown to his bride to be, she was standing on his land, when she lit up, smiled and said 'Yes Gabe … I'll gladly be your wife', before running round and round in circles whooping. Gabe was over the moon and

had encouraged her to return to Wales to spend Christmas with her parents and to celebrate the happy news, and at the same time she would sell her cottage and her painted furniture business. This would leave Gabe free to do something he'd been planning, as a surprise for Seraphina. He roped in all his friends, who were happy to help, especially when they heard Gabe was getting married, and they built a log cabin in four long hard weeks. Gabe was a gifted carpenter and a natural architect, having a real love of creating something special and lasting, something that would be appreciated long after he was gone. The job was tough, it was Winter and they all worked day and night to finish the little house in time for the New Millennium Eve, when Seraphina was to have come back from Wales. Gabe never lived to see her set foot on their cherished dream of a ranch.

Almost there now, driving further away from civilization, Seraphina felt the remoteness of where she was intensely, 'If only Max my dog was with me, he'd guard me', she thought. Tears came next and by the time she reached the ranch her face was red and puffy and her hands were shaking. 'Holy Shit, I hope you're watching out for me, Gabe, because I'm feeling way out of my depth right now,' she mumbled under her breath, as she turned a last steep corner and looked straight into the heart of Turtle Creek Ranch. More tears now, tears of pure relief and tired joy. There before her was her dream world, a Hill Country delight. It was one of those defining moments in Seraphina's life when for once, just once, her unshakable and incurable optimism, was bang-on. Something wonderful and good had come out of something terrible and sad.

The little front door was painted faded red, with a blacksmith-made, round metal handle and a black steel escutcheon keyhole. Before turning the key she stepped back to really look at the little house. A stone chimney exposed on the side stacked its way up in a natural way. The same was repeated on the opposite side. Gabe had built a 'double cabin', each side with its own hearth and a 'dog-trot' running through the middle, like an open-plan corridor and a little porch on the front and a different one out back. Everything under one shared shingle roof, chunks of split burr oak neatly laid out and fastened with skill, not nails or screws. The crafted roof, held down with long poles stretched across, ensuring a wind and rain-proof space. The cabin was log, solid oak log, with dove-tail corners and the front had been overlaid with 'clapboard' which gave the best of both worlds of style. A log cabin on the one hand and a pretty painted New England house on the other. The front was whitewashed, contrasting pleasingly with the red door and the painted pale blue window frames. The hands that built this house belonged to a unique, skilled artist. Another side to Gabe. Seraphina took the key out of her pocket and pointed it towards the industrial-sized keyhole, assuming it was going to be a stiff, two-handed struggle to turn the key. The lock bolt clunked open with a superior precision and unexpected soft heavy ease, opening inwards, nudging a yawning screen door wide open. It was dark inside as all the shutters were closed. Instinctively, Seraphina walked straight ahead along the 'dog-trot' to the back door and read the bolts like Braille. Like a safe in the Bank of England the bolts clunked open, she pulled the door inwards and stepped outside. The sight was staggering and beautiful and extreme. Tilting gently down and away from the back porch step, a floral meadow lay drenched in colour, red, orange, blue, white, yellow, silver, magenta, pink, mauve and mustard. Tumbling onto the tiny wonky shore of a tingling, twinkling creek running just below the house, flanking it, in its higgledy piggledy horizontal. Betsy and Leopold, the errant mules, grazed peacefully in a little paddock on the side. Cricket, the one-eyed goat was tethered, and nibbling round the round-pen with the look of Napoleon about him, with his bandaged eye. Seven or eight longhorn cows were roaming in the distance, some lying with legs tucked under, chewing the cud. Seraphina was standing under the huge oak tree gazing down and up and across the Texas Hill Country at last. The blue, blue clear sky took her breath away as she gasped 'Oh Gabe .. I just died and went to Heaven, sweet thing.' The scent, the absolute signature-scent of where she was, sent her smiling uncontrollably, lolling her head back

looking up,up,up through the leaves and branches of the massive tree. Squirrels scampered and darted, birds tweeted, and as if to welcome her personally, a great pink tawny armadillo pottered past.
She thought about Max, her beloved dog and could just imagine him bounding around and jumping full-pelt into the creek. She had a sudden image of him leaping like a stag on their last walk, before she left him. A lifetime of living in towns and watching too much television had made her cautious on walks in the countryside alone, she knew she couldn't live that way here, so she gave in and surrendered to the risk. She decided then and there, that the only time she would look over her shoulder or scan the horizon, would be to take in the view. The conscious decision made her feel liberated and truly in the hands of destiny. The spring-fed creek was the size of a real river to Seraphina, and it was overflowing with fish, perch, bass and catfish. Unable to wait, unwilling to rush things anymore, instead of unpacking and exploring further, Seraphina went fishing that sunny lunchtime in the middle of nowhere. She needed to kick-back, the last few days of living the emotional roller coaster on nerves and adrenaline had fried her batteries well and truly. The only frying going on that afternoon was the fresh succulent fish she cooked up in a jiff on the new camping stove at the creek's edge. Fed and slowly rejuvenating, Seraphina threw open all the

little shutters and marvelled at the simple, scrubbed homely interior. Two chairs and a small wooden table in one room. One iron bedstead in the other. Both stone hearths were swept clean and piled neatly beside each, there was a mound of expertly chopped logs. The walls were bare except for the shapes of the round oak logs making them. There was a cedar ladder in one corner, hewn with the bark still on in places. Seraphina clambered up into the comfortable roof space. A huge, stuffed, antlered stag-head with glinting eyes hung in the apex of the gable, Bambi with attitude, a real trophy. Piles of brown, white-tailed deer hides lay on the decked floor in one corner. The space was clean swept and the only piece of furniture was a small bookcase with one book. It was the autobiography of the first man who walked on the moon. Seraphina climbed off the top of the ladder to stand and reach the book. She opened the front cover and it was inscribed by the man himself, 'Gabe, thanks for the great day's huntin', wish I had your life. Neil Armstrong', a photo of Earth Rising was the bookmarker.

A sound she'd only heard in old Westerns broke the muffled peace in the splendid roof-space. Popping the book back on the dinky bookcase, she squirrelled back down the rough ladder and out the back door, to the pounding, and sight of horses galloping through the floral meadow, followed by one lone rider expertly wielding a bull-whip. Like a molten jigsaw, they swept round in a circle right in front of Seraphina, then fitted and settled in the right place – Gabe's round pen. One 'Yee Haa' was all it took to recognise a woman's voice. 'That must be my new neighbour, Eve Buchanan, bringing Gabe's horses back', Seph thought with awe. With a final flourish of flamboyant behaviour, E. B. as everyone called her, latched the round-pen gate and hurtled up the meadow, screeching to a super halt on horseback, her nostrils flared, and without taking a breath said, 'Don't we live in a terrible place and ain't you miraculous!' Seraphina introduced herself.

'Hell, I know who you are Miss Seraphina. The whole town's talking about you. They're laying bets on how much you're gonna git for this place when you sell up.'

'Oh I won't be selling up', assured Seraphina.

'We'll see Miss Seraphina, we'll see.'

An awkward silence prompted Seraphina to start fiddling with her waist band. 'Thanks for taking care of the horses, now how much do I owe you?',

'We'll call it $500.00 shall we?'

'Yes of course, quite right.' With that she produced the stash from her trousers and handed over some money. E.B. looked at Seraphina with a scrunched up face. 'You gotta gun?'

'No no I don't have a gun.'

'Here take mine.' E.B. threw a rifle spinning into the air and amazingly, Seraphina caught it like a

good ‘un. Next, E.B. made a spectacular rearing turn on her black horse, calling over her shoulder, as she galloped off, ‘I’ll pick you up at 11 am sharp. Tomorrow we’re gonna buy you a gun, Miss Seraphina, one with bows on if you like.’
‘Righty ho’ sputtered Seraphina choking on the cloud of dust left behind by her careering new neighbour.

It was early evening by the time Seraphina had unloaded the car and carried all she had into the little house. She was dying to light a fire in the hearth but it was a warm May day and the room was naturally cosy. For the first time in her life she had found herself in a place that fitted her like a beautiful, soft kid glove, custom made for her. Gabe was all around her, watching over her, loving her, she felt. The sadness of knowing he was dead was hard to take but it was as if his ‘presence’ sustained her, protected her from feeling pain anymore. Someone looking in from the outside, might have seen that as sad, unhealthy even. A loving woman ‘going to waste’, living on her memory of the love of her life. She felt she had him back now. The little ranch house was her bliss, her destiny. The house symbolized everything she ever wanted. Protected and safe and shared with her forever partner, Gabe, a ghost. Dismantling her whole life in Wales in record time was easy because in her soul she was running, running back to Gabe’s arms. A profound need to be held and

nurtured was quenched by returning to his life, and the life he'd made for her. She lit the wood-burning stove in the small lean-to kitchen at the back of the house and unpacked her brand-new cowboy coffee pot. It was identical to the one they used camping, a mini percolator, a simple thing that worked perfectly.
'Right then, I'd better go and meet the menagerie,' she said out loud, downing the cup of coffee from her brand-new mug with barbed wire patterns printed on.

She skipped down the floral slope, too inviting not to, and strolled up to Betsy and Leopold, who were happily standing with their big old heads over the rail. 'Enormous ears you've got', Seraphina was patting the mules and stroking their shining huge, donkey-horsey waggling ears. She was captivated and glad she'd gone to the trouble of reading the massive tome, How To Handle A Mule. They charmed her instantly, nuzzling and licking her hand, sniffing her hair. Leopold rested his thick whiskery lips on top of her head and took a deep breath in through his nostrils. He liked the smell of her. Feeling left out, Cricket was bleating and tugging at the little tether keeping him in a perfect round limitation. The ground he'd been on all day looked as if a small spaceship had landed and taken off again.
'Hello Cricket,' she called over, walking towards him, 'allow me to introduce myself ', she stroked

his efficient nose and pulled up the spike holding the tether and moved him on to fresh pasture. This pleased the one-eyed goat and he calmed down and went straight back to grazing. Seraphina had read all sorts of things about goats being zany and delinquent. 'I don't know what all those books were talking about, you seem very civilized to me,' she cooed to Cricket.

The horses were settled in the round-pen, all five of them with ears pricked forward, looking politely at Seraphina. She'd brought a head collar down and was going to lead them, one at a time, up to the barn across from the house. The whole exercise went smoothly, a Christian bunch of horses if ever there was such a thing. Standing in their individual stalls she drew each of them a fresh bucket of water from the neat little holding tank close by. They were all thirsty and calmly grateful. Next, she opened a door through the barn partition and found what she was looking for, an immaculately stacked full hay barn. Clambering up to the top, really enjoying herself, she threw down a few bales of sweet-smelling meadow hay. The horses clomped about a bit and snickered for the tea-time treat, each one getting a swatch. There are few sounds on earth more pleasing and restoring to the soul, than a contented horse munching hay. She sat on a bale out of sight, just listening, with her chin resting in her hands leaning on her knees.

Back at the house she organized the kerosene lamps and checked a couple of old oil lamps already there, ready for later when it would get dark. There was mains electricity in that area, stretched out on towering poles into the distance but it wasn't officially connected to the house. Gabe had 'tapped' the overhead cable ingeniously, so that enough 'juice' leaked out 'accidentally', powering a couple of lights and a hot water heater to take a bath. The bathroom was in another small lean-to at the back and was neat as a new pin.

As if she'd always lived there, Seraphina prepared an easy beef casserole and popped it in the tiny wood burning oven, in a delightful red enamelled dish with the lid on. She stoked up the fire and went back to the barn. '...... eeney meeney miney mo .... ', she had no idea which horse was which, so taking the first bridle, she identified the owner by a process of elimination, trying it on each patient horse, like the slipper in Cinderella. 'You shall go ....', tugging hard to squeeze the wrong bridle on the wrong horse, 'umm ... maybe not ....' Three horses later, 'Ah ha…you shall go to the ball'. It was Chaz who had the honour of taking Seraphina on her first tour of Turtle Creek Ranch as she rode the fence line that evening.

A hand-made cedar post and rail, fence surrounded all three hundred and fifty various acres. A labour of love and a special thing to behold, not a break or a wobbly, fallen down piece, anywhere. She knew it was a dying craft and felt the need to jump off Chaz and touch the hewn barky rail with her hands – it was tactile and scented and unwavering. Gabe was a preserver of the natural world he'd once inhabited and his 'fence' was there to show a boundary, not to keep one. Not too high and not to dense, ensuring any wild animal could get through, under or over it. Back on Chaz now, she rode in the divine sunset, surrounded by deer and swooping flocks of birds going to roost for the night. Fireflies made a silent firework display in one spot and she stared in wonder. It was almost dark when she got back, hastily lighting the lamps in the house, she returned to the barn and turned the horses out to graze for the night. The paddock gate firmly closed, the horses knowing it was free time squealed and bucked and rolled in Gods' earth. That night, there was no fear left in her, no sadness on the surface, either. Swept into the landscape and enveloped by its majesty, she happily ate supper in her tiny log cabin, in the middle of nowhere.

Chapter Ten

Seraphina slept like an angel that first night, except for when she woke up bolt upright, saying, 'Oh my God .. Cricket.' Running barefoot through the floral meadow, swinging a Tilley lamp, at three in the morning, in her pyjamas, she tracked down the little post-operative demoralized goat. She led him back up the meadow to the barn and opened a stable door, frantically cooing and chucking down a straw bed. With Cricket safe in the stable, she ran back to the house to boil clean water and read the instructions left by the town vet. A small feed with the antibiotics and anti-inflammatory mixed in and a clean change of bandage, after bathing the stitched furry socket in boric acid powder dissolved in warm water. That done, he looked awful, de-horned and all bandaged up as Seraphina stroked his nose. She'd read the Goat Husbandry book thoroughly and wondered how old he was, so looking in his mouth, she examined his teeth, 'Ummm ..... I think you're either two or twelve ... ummm, not sure really', as she kissed his bony head and was rewarded with a gentle butt. Satisfied that Cricket would live, she headed back to the house. It was 4 am and her jet-lag meant she was wide awake and starving. Soon she had the wood fired up in the kitchen stove and the radio on pinging out Blue Grass guitar and a lovely voice. Ham and eggs and hot chocolate sent her back to bed where she had a deep perfect sleep.

She was woken by her new neighbour tooting the truck horn, impatient to go gun shopping. E.B. must have been around sixty-five, though it was difficult to be accurate. Years of living in the great outdoors had weathered her feminine complexion into a brown, freckled, part of the scenery. Jet black eyes, like a friendly minx, intelligently beady. Fit as a flea, slim hipped, the daily exercise of her lone lady rancher life, keeping her in remarkable working order. There wasn't much an experienced cowboy could do which she couldn't. There was plenty though, that she could do, to leave a cowboy standing. Her spread was next door to Seraphina's, about 500 acres. E.B. had known Gabe for years and it was because of that she was keeping a helpful eye on Seraphina. Her unspoken mission, was helping Seraphina to learn everything she needed to survive as a lone lady rancher. The whole thing was regarded as 'pure entertainment', better 'an cable TV!' by E.B., besides which, it was giving her new status and kudos in the local watering hole, as she divulged her not too unkind, daily bulletins about how Miss Seraphina was 'stacking up', to half of Droversville. 'I'll just be a minute', shouted Seraphina to the waiting new neighbour as she quickly dressed, locked the house and threw some hay in for Cricket. Off they went to the gun shop. The sensation of driving away from her new ranch, bumping along on the dirt track was wonderful, knowing she was returning to all that glorious future and fun. Excited about the prospect of her very own gun, she'd remembered to bring her passport for the required I.D. needed for a gun license. She chirped away to E.B. telling her how she'd ridden the fence line on Chaz and how 'utterly wonderful' the little ranch was and how she felt like 'the luckiest woman on earth'. E.B. was pleased that Miss Miraculous, as she now called her, had the spunk to saddle up a fresh new horse and go for it, out into the hills, alone. It surprised her actually, and she put the fact that Seraphina hadn't been bucked off and left for dead down to 'beginner's luck.'

The shopping trip went smoothly and was over in a few minutes. Seraphina saw the gun she wanted and walked straight up to the counter saying, 'I'll have that one, thank you.' E.B. was taken aback for the second time that morning and when they'd done the licensing paperwork she drove home with a, 'Well what have we got here then?' expression. Seraphina not noticing, just humming quietly away to herself, holding her gun across her lap in its brand-new carry case with bows on. E.B pulled up outside her new neighbour's log cabin and turning off the noisy engine expressed her deep sadness at Gabe's untimely death. Seraphina was grateful and bravely smiled at her new friend. It was not an easy conversation but it was appreciated.

There was something about Seraphina and horses in particular. Her knack, which it surely was, was unexpected to others, but not to her. Her mother always said it was because she was descended from Welsh Drovers, who some believed were the original Cowboys. She knew early on she could connect with a horse, ride and stride and be good with one. On, off or just by its side. She could handle a horse and looked special when she rode. Gabe had noticed this the first time he took her trail-riding at the Dude Ranch. On a later outing with Gabe the horse she was riding was in danger of being kicked by another horse, who had boxed her onto the edge of a rocky bluff. The hairy moment contrived accidentally by holiday riders on fresh horses. In a heartbeat, without blinking, Seraphina squeezed the right places on her old-timer cow pony, who was perky that morning with a real pilot astride, for a change. Rising to the signal, the old horse bunched himself up and steadily he walked backwards over the edge of the shallow bluff and stopped when asked, like Spiderman on a wall. Seraphina, still giving him his head, with an easy rein, 'leaned' him off-side and made a kissing sound with her lips, the only cue he needed. Horse and rider skittered back up the bluff at a straight diagonal and took off from nowhere to a safe landing. Gabe loved that Seraphina could handle a horse, the equalizer, a foundation stone of untaintable mutual respect.

Meanwhile, back at the ranch, there was plenty to do. Seraphina scurrying about like an important bird making her Home Sweet Home nest. Pretty curtains were up and tied back with ribbons. Little scatter rugs decorated the old timber floors. An American quilt adorned the old bed, with a brand-new mattress underneath. Mirrors and charming pictures hung on the walls with a drifting mobile of bucking horses dangling from the ceiling in the living room. She'd been to the Charity Welfare shop and picked out some small bits of old furniture, which she'd hand-painted in an oversized gingham design in pale blue and cream. Decorative painted furniture suited the wonderful exposed log interior of the cabin. Scented candles and the old chiming French clock on the mantel above the big hearth added a final touch of home comfort.

Gracing the stone chimney breast supported on brackets, was Seraphina's new 'gun with bows on', a rifle, a good vintage Winchester .30-.30 carbine repeater. A famously perfect saddle gun, compact with a rapid rate of fire. If she missed the running rabbit the first time she could have another crack in a millisecond. The gun had been a reliable favourite of many a cowboy in the past and, it was safe to say that Seraphina was definitely over-gunned. Too much fire-power is never a good thing for a novice hunter or a rabbit, for that matter.

The day to day running of her life was varied and fun. Seraphina was preserving a little ranch world all of her own, with Gabe by her side. After all, she slept in his bed and ate at his table, she rode his horses. She drove his pick-up and took care of his cows and mules. She even wore his hat, left behind on the hook by the door. What she had really done was lock herself in his world alone, her guard dropped. Her bleeding heart was healed and renewed. She'd opened herself up, trusting and depending on the love she had for Gabe. All the pain and difficulties and tragedy of her own life so far, like many other people's lives, was subdued beneath the surface because she was happy inside and in a place she wanted to be. In reality, Seraphina hadn't faced up to Gabe's death. As each different, living day passed, she got to know every square inch of Gabe's house, all the detail she'd missed in the beginning. The way he'd taken such care over the building of that double cabin, because he knew she was coming. As if he was showing her every day how much he loved her. The beautiful hand-made doors and window frames, the rocking chair and swinging bench on the porches. The heart-shaped cut-outs on the porch frame out front. The placing of the house on a floral meadow. The safety of the house, ensuring a woman alone would be protected. Gabe had almost geared it perfectly. Seraphina was kept so busy running the little 'outfit', not too big, not too small, a girl-size ranch, that she slept like a log and never felt lonely. Just enough contact with the outside world but not enough to pierce the bubble she thrived in. It was as if Gabe knew her suffering at being parted from him and understood it because his suffering was equal. His love for her was equal. Turtle Creek Ranch was the 'dream place' they had envisaged and talked about together, round the campfire out in the Hill Country. Each one making a suggestio to the other, right down to the round pen. Seraphina was living in the place they had imagined together. The house became her life blood, somewhere she would stay forever and grow old in and get carried out of with her boots on, one day. That certainty and sense of belonging, was good for Seraphina and long overdue. In her early thirties now and after all that she'd been through, she felt she was done with striving and struggling. She was ready to just be and live in peace.

E.B. was tough as old boots with a big heart underneath, she knew the truth about Seraphina's plight, as she viewed it, and was moved by it. She remembered Gabe working all hours to build the cabin. She would ride out to see him and joke and pull his leg. 'This ain't no cowboy's house you're building. This is a lovebirds' nest.' Gabe ignoring E.B. and laughing as he painstakingly carried on smoothing the porch rail by hand, with fine sand-paper. 'Who is she Gabe? Where is she?', Gabe stopped his work for a moment and leaned on the rail. 'Her name is Seraphina, it means angel. This house, this land, is my gift to her and I'd be mighty honoured if you'd come to our wedding.'
'Well I'll be. You betcha Gabe … why I wouldn't miss the sight of you finally walking up that aisle for all the tea in China.'
The memory made E.B. wince, she understood her new neighbours' pain, she'd experienced it herself.

Seraphinas' love for Gabe was so deep and everlasting, that her comfort was to climb out of his bed in the morning and place her feet where his had been and yearn in his space.

The birds were tweeting and the perfume of ripe melons filled the air, 'Now this I gotta see,' said E.B. leaning against the barn door, one leg crossed in front of the other, arms folded. Shaking her head from side to side, looking at Seraphina and wondering if Miss Miraculous needed to get out more. Seraphina was dressed for riding and ranch chores as she always was, chaps, spurs, boots, cuffs, but this time she was wearing a contraption around her chest, a sort of Heath Robinson device, which allowed her to ride with a dozen eggs held in a neat unbreakable row, close to her front. She'd saddled up Mimi the rearing horse, the same horse who had nearly got Seraphina killed the day before when she rode over to E.B's for her first lesson in rounding up the young stock and getting them branded. Now Seraphina could not abide a rearing horse and the only reason she hadn't sold Mimi on day one, was because the mare was characterful and interesting and bomb-proof, unaffected by gunshots when Seraphina was riding in the middle of nowhere whilst firing the Winchester. Anyhow, the horse would, just for the hell of it, with no warning, rear up and rear up, then fling down and kick her hind legs in the air. Dangerous as hell, especially on a tall bony horse that was old enough to know better. The possibility of the mare toppling over backwards on top of a rider, was real and could split a human pelvis in two. The day before Seraphina had hit the deck and had bruised her ribs, the horse just an inch away from crashing over backwards and crushing her. Seraphina had concluded she'd give the mare one last chance, before selling her on as 'not a novice ride'.

The mare was feeling spicy that sunny morning and looking forward to some uncontrolled rearing up before tiring herself and behaving for the rest of the day. Seraphina could always feel when it was going to happen because the mare would curl her back under the saddle. That morning Seraphina was ready, primed, and quite looking forward to administering the last chance old Welsh remedy. 'Whoomph', up the horse went, on hind legs with Seraphina like a fairy on top of a teetering tall Christmas tree, standing in the stirrups on tip-toe, defying gravity, 'Wham!', crashed the raw egg, right between the horse's ears, as Seraphina smashed it down, with all her might, on the animal's skull. 'Whoomph', 'Wham!', 'Woomph', 'Wham!', 'Whoomph','Wham! Wham! Wham!!' Mimi the mare, thinking the dripping eggs were her own blood pouring down all over her face and eyes and nostrils, from her 'smashed' skull, stopped rearing.

‘Right then, time for breakfast I think. Omelette ok?’, smiled Seraphina as she hopped off her horse and tethered the contrite animal to Gabes’ hitching rail. ‘Yup I reckon omelette should just about hit the spot.’, drawled E.B. once she’d managed to reclaim her dropped jaw. Standing over the stove in the little lean-to kitchen at the back, Seraphina took a clean frying pan and broke the six eggs that were left. This was a good sign, she knew if it took more than half a dozen eggs smashed over the skull of her horse, then Mimi was looking at a Winchester between the eyes. With breakfast whisked up and cooking in the pan, she undid the Heath Robinson contraption and hung it on a spoon hook in the corner. E.B. was sitting at the hand-painted gingham patterned table for two, lapping it up. ‘You know what, Miss Miraculous? Gabe would have loved this little table, he would have especially loved to be sittin’ at it, eating breakfast with you … I know that for certain.’ Seraphina smiled and swallowed a rush of emotion at the mention of his name and busied herself serving the omelette. E.B. filled the void with more on the matter. ‘Man, that cowboy loved you like no other, you were his joy, his inspiration in building this little house. He built it for you. I miss him, he was a decent man and loved you to the end.’ Seraphina, unable to speak, placed her hand over E.B.’s resting on the table. She sat down and ate the omelette, salty now as silent tears ran down her cheek and got swallowed like they always were.

'Now E.B., apart from rounding up and branding my young stock, we've got peach and melon harvesting to get through. Do you have a good jam recipe? And do you think anyone wants my lovely melons?'
'Well I shall be mighty disappointed if *someone* out there don't want your lovely melons.' The alternative meaning to that statement had them howling and holding their stomachs for laughing.

Chapter Eleven

E.B. was close to becoming everyone's main source of entertainment at the local watering hole, what with her hot-off-the press news bulletins on Seraphina. The Drover, as it was called, was a tin shack draped in camouflage netting and khaki tarpaulins, spiked with the occasional white bare-bone, long-horn skull, the massive horns twizzling skyward at jaunty angles. Purposely giving the venue a huntin', shootin', fishin' look, for the type of individuals it wanted to attract. All the local Unrestricted Ones hung out there as regulars.
'My, my .. Miss Miraculous is over-gunned and over here. Watch out boys! Why she made me an omelette on a horse's head this very morning!'

Drawling chuckles came from the mixed bag of Hill Country folk, followed by faces expectant for more. 'Come on E.B., don't keep us in suspense ... How did she pan-out, rigging up old Leopold and Betsy, for that sunset hayride she was hankerin' after?'

'Oh right now it's still just talk. She's kinda skirting round those big old mules, not sure what to make of 'em.'

More friendly laughter. Even though most in that bar didn't really know the intrepid Welsh lady rancher, they were developing a caring nosey affection for her, men and women alike. If they passed her in Walmart buying her groceries they politely stepped aside and touched their hats. They knew so much more about her than she did about them, completely unaware as she was to the fact she was the butt of all jokes, however friendly, at The Drovers.

E.B. went on, with her best stage whisper, 'You know she even thinks that the spirit of White Cloud, a Warrior Chief, might be lookin' out for her.' No one laughed at that. Instead they changed the subject a little and got to talking about other things in their usual way.

Seraphinas' crash course in ranching, courtesy of E.B. was relentless, challenging and daunting. One typical evening, Seraphina sat on her back porch step, stiff and aching from the stupendous wrestling she'd been practising most of the day, with E.B. coaching ringside.

'That's it! Hold him down! Twist his head! Hold him!'

'I'm trying! I'm trying! Shit and bloody bollocks!'

Seraphina was learning the rumbustious art of cutting out a steer, roping him, tripping him and tying his legs in a knot, before twisting his head back-to-front like a bovine owl.

'That's it! Now 'Crop the right' and 'Swallow-fork' the left! No! No! you just did 'em wrong way round!'

'Well it's too bloody late now! If I Crop them any more he's not going to have any ears left is he? He's going to be the first bloody earless steer in the whole of flaming Texas!'

The 'marking', by cutting a shape into an animal's ear is a tricky business and takes practice and skill and superhuman strength, if you're a Welsh shopkeeper who's never done it before. Wielding a sharp little knife, Seraphina had been taught that morning, using some old linoleum from a pile in the tack room.

'Now, never cut the ear from the outside in, we're not talking about cheese here. Them steers' ears are tricky if you don't start the split from a good way in.'

Covered in the steer's blood after being dragged around the round-pen on her stomach, with the sharp knife unsafely between her teeth, Seraphina let go of the rope and clambered up to sit on the rail, delicately removing the blade from her mouth.

‘You know what E.B.? That work’s a bit dangerous and I think I’ve had enough for a minute, I need to catch my breath ..’

‘Miss Miraculous, you’ve got some guts you know that?’

Both laughing now, two women, loving a ‘mans’ job.

‘Anyways’ went on E.B. ‘Tall Jake’s over at mine, with his crew and they’re comin’ over here, to do all your little herd too.’

‘Oh that’s great what a relief .. I’ll pay them of course’, Seraphina was still gasping and glugging from her water bottle, spattered with blood mixed in with earth mixed in with sweat and tears.

‘No need for that .. those boys are coming for the pure curiosity of meeting Miss Miraculous.’

Climbing down from the fence rail she’d been sitting on, and deftly cleaning the sharp penknife she’d been wielding with such well-meant unprofessionalism she said ‘Ummm .. well I’d better get baking then.’

You know ‘Jake’s the handsomest, straightest finest man that I have ever met in my life.’

Seraphina scrutinized E.B., thoughtfully, trying to remember where she had heard those words before… ‘Heck E.B. that’s exactly how Buffalo Bill Cody was described a century and a half ago, by someone who really knew him … as ‘the handsomest, straightest finest man, that I have ever met in my life.’

'Well I'll be.' said E.B. with uncharacteristic nonchalance.

'I grew up with an amazing painting of him on my bedroom wall, my grandfather gave it to me and I'm so attached to it, I brought it with me, it's in the house.'

'That's right, you showed it to me remember? When we were sorting out the deer hides in the upstairs roof space and you said, almost wistfully, as I recall, staring at the painting, that he would be the only man that could compete with Gabe for your affection.'

Seraphina was intrigued, 'Don't tell me Jake's got gorgeous flowing locks and a divine silken moustache as well?'

E.B. chuckled, 'That's for me to know and for you to find out, I guess.'

'Yeh right', Seraphina laughed, 'You'll be telling me next that he has a 'magnificent presence and physique', he's 'an unerring shot', a 'perfect horseman' and that he's dressed head to toe in heavenly fringed buckskin!'

E.B. gave Seraphina a sage look and enigmatic smile.

'I don't believe a word of it E.B. If Tall Jake turns out to be a twenty-first Century Bill Cody, then I'm Calamity Jane.'

'Well if making you Calamity Jane gets you to shoot straight, we'll have achieved somethin' here today, God willing.'

'God's got nothing to do with it.'

'Oh Miss Miraculous, you crease me up .. you do really.'
Both of them were howling with laughter and with that Seraphina ran through the meadow and got the home-fires burning in the kitchen. She pulled out a big old bake stone and slung it on the stove to heat up. By the time it had reached the perfect temperature she had a hundred Welsh Cakes rolled out and cut out, in perfect rounds and started cooking up a delicious mound just like her Mum always had when Seraphina was a child. The smell of raisins and flour and butter and nutmeg was too delicious for words.
Tall Jake's boys had every steer and heifer ear-marked in milliseconds and had still not met Miss Miraculous. Sheepishly they dawdled up to the back porch on horseback, lured by the unfamiliar aroma of something they hadn't tried before. Those boys cleared a mountain of delicious warm Welsh Cakes in a methodical wholly polite manner, and just stared at Seraphina while doing so.
'Well, thanks so much for doing the ear-marking, I'm terribly grateful.'
'It was a pleasure Mam, you be sure an' tell ole E.B. if there's anything we can help with again, don't forget now.' said one of the crew.
Lovely as those cowboys were, none of them came close to her romantic hero, her namesake, William F. Cody. Seraphina was annoyed at her disappointment because it made her feel disloyal to Gabe. She sat down on the back porch step,

self-conscious all of a sudden, a shyness took hold of her and bending her head she looked down and undid her spurs, feelings of tiredness and loneliness made her beautiful blue eyes sting. Deep in thought she was unaware of his presence, on horseback standing in the cool water of Turtle Creek, opposite her, square on. She slowly looked up and caught her breath, the reflection of the light from the river was shining up straight into his face and lighting it up like 'some kind of an aura' not quite believing what she was seeing, she stared, transfixed … 'I have met a … god in my life' she whispered.

Remembering her manners she walked towards him, the plate of Welsh Cakes she held in her hand was wobbling all over the place. Jake was bare chested and, his muscular tanned torso joined seamlessly with the fringed buck skin leggings he wore. He dismounted and steadied the plate, 'Pardon me Mam ..', as he took a clean shirt out of his saddle bag and put it on, 'My other shirt got messed up ear-marking that little herd you have.'

Seraphina blurted how grateful she was and Jake turned to face her, tucking in his shirt, looking directly into her eyes, 'Miss Mirac … I mean Miss Cody, Mam, it is an honour to assist you in all things, anyway I can. I'm Jake Buchanan.' and he shook her worn out hand.

'Oh My God .. Buffalo Bill Cody has come for a Welsh Cake.', she yipped in her head. Seraphina fluttered her eyelashes before blushing deep

crimson, mortified that a feminine instinct had well and truly got the better of her.
'Do have a Welsh Cake … if you'd like one that is … I mean they might not be something you would really like …. b.. b .. but …', Jake took one, warm, scented cake from the plate and ate it, chewing every mouthful with care and thought, looking at Seraphina. He smiled a deep lovely smile and thanked her. Climbing back on their horses, Jake and the real cowboys headed out and one said to the other, 'Man, those Cakes of Wales were somethin' else..'
Seraphina busied herself tidying the kitchen and humming 'Oh What A Beautiful Mornin'. She kept seeing Jake's face in her mind, his eyes and mouth and the way he spoke.
E.B. was stood in the doorway, 'Why I do believe that song your're hummin' was made famous in that movie … what was it now? Oh that's right Calamity Jane '
'Fetch the guns E.B. I'm gonna shoot straight today.'

****

The summer evenings at the ranch were like Heaven on Earth. The sunsets and the deer and the balmy warm scented atmosphere were good medicine for Seraphina. She'd often sit on the swinging bench on the little back porch and write letters to her Mum and Dad, and they loved passing on all the 'clecs' to friends and neighbours. Her Mum was a great letter writer and one arrived from Wales every week without fail for Seraphina to prise out of her real American mailbox. Gabe had made the cutest mailbox on a stick that she'd ever seen, all painted up with a cowboy feeding a pair of doves perched on his arm. That particular evening she wrote to give the go ahead for Max, her beloved dog, to be sent out to live with her on the ranch. She could hardly wait and neither could Max.

Her inherited ranch was costing money and its only income was from taking a few cattle to the stockyards for auction for not very many dollars. An unwieldy business for a lone lady rancher with a small 'outfit' and emotionally draining, waving goodbye to Blossom and Buttercup and Bill and Ben the little steers with hardly any ears left.

'Them steers sure got funny lookin' ears', commented the auctioneer to Seraphina, to which she replied, 'Oh that's completely normal in...um.. Australia! … it's called the 'Koala Crop'.

Seraphina needed to move with the times and diversify, a natural entrepreneur, whenever an idea came to her, no matter how crazy sounding, she'd jot it down on a notepad.

Chillies – now growing chillies was big business down in Mexico and Seraphina had met a retired couple at a coffee morning who knew everything there was to know about chilli farming. She'd been invited by the Restricted Ones, the ones who lived in gated communities, in enormous mansions, and weren't allowed to hang their laundry on a washing-line in their own yard. The invitation had come about when she was shopping in Droversville at a designer cowboy-type-person boutique. Treating herself to a 'Brighton' handbag to die for, with matching belt, her British accent had attracted everyone's nosey attention.

'You're not from around here then?' enquired an immaculately kitted out Restricted lady.

'No, I'm from Wales actually but live here now, over at Turtle Creek.'

The lady and her husband exchanged approving glances.

'So you're a wet-back' exclaimed the husband, to jolly tittering from the other wealthy shoppers, meaning she was someone who'd just got off the boat.

'I guess you could say that. I've only been here a few months but I feel very at home now, I must say.'

So one thing led to another and the next day Seraphina had an eleven o'clock appointment for coffee at a lovely gated ranch estate, Tierra Cindy, on the outskirts of Droversville.

The gates themselves were magnificent in a Rococco/Baroque sort of a way and looked all the more incongruous because they were flanked with large painted signs depicting a bandit with a scarf tied in such a way, that only

the shifty eyes could be seen. The sign read 'BEWARE 24 HOUR SURVEILLANCE.'
Sure enough Seraphina was 'greeted' quickly and super-efficiently, not because she was coming for coffee but because she was driving Gabe's dented old pick-up, with the repaired door not resprayed yet to match the rest. Once her identity had been established, questioned and verified over a walkie-talkie, she was handed a super-efficient map, printed and very professional. She had the heady navigational task of driving a hundred yards and turning left. Once in, she enjoyed a splendid morning chatting about her life as a lady rancher and her need to diversify. She discovered early on, that most of the '... just simple retired folks, is all.' were in fact ex-CIA Agents and spent Special Forces Operatives. They had all retired to The Hill Country 'coincidentally', and enjoyed a real rapport in their gated world. The security arrangements were all organised and operated by the spectacularly over-qualified residents on a voluntary basis. Brand new shiny trucks were purchased out of their communal donated fund, each with satellite navigation systems and a flashing light facility on the roof. They had set up their fail-safe walkie-talkie system which only allowed code names to be used, their old military call-signs. The introductions at the coffee morning sounded like a Who's Who from Top Gun.

'Now Seraphina, let me introduce you, couple by couple. This is Hellfire and his wife Viper, over here we have Scorpion and her husband Ice, next we have Juice and his lovely new wife Mixer and last but not least, Chilli One and Chilli Two. Oh! I almost forgot, I'm Widow and my old man's Blue.'

Seraphina was offered a homemade blueberry muffin and the man chatting to someone next to her said, 'Nuke the lot of them that's the way.' and she didn't think he was referring to his wife's baking.

The couple who owned a zillion dollars-worth of chilli plantation in Mexico, Chilli One and Two, got very excited at Seraphina's need to diversify and said they'd be happy to look over her little ranch and see if it was suitable for some kind of micro-specialist chilli growing operation.

Seraphina could just see the advertising slogan, 'These aren't just any chillies – these are Hilly-Billy Chillies' and she wondered if she could get the buyer from Marks & Spencer over to do a deal.

The next hour flew by with the unusually skilled, inquisitive conversation and Seraphina felt sure she hadn't told so many complete strangers, so much about herself, in such a short time, ever before.

'Well I've had a lovely time, thank you all so much for making me so welcome. See you all tomorrow evening then, around eight … that's right ..The Drover.... you can't miss it ... it's the one with the skulls on the outside. Sorry?... Oh yes yes .... then we'll all go up to my place for a sunset mule ride in the old wagon ... asta la vista ....bye for now.'

Chapter Twelve

Driving back through town from Tierra Cindy Ranch that hot lunchtime, Seraphina passed the dance hall she and Gabe used to visit. It was still there looking spruce and popular. Their dancing was something else, Gabe having a feel for the music which was a real gift. He danced like a dream, holding Seraphina with his warm body and taking her smooching and spinning with a professional ease. She hardly thought about the steps, she simply flowed in the wake of her wonderful guide. The up-tempo numbers had her twirling and letting go and spinning back into Gabe's arms, twinkling and smiling in a feminine way. The slow dances were truly memorable for Seraphina, and thinking about those times brought round hot tears to her eyes. Gabe would project an intense energy when holding her close and dancing slow. Her heart rate increased and her breathing became shallow and expectant, as Gabe would literally melt the final bars of the song into a tender, lingering kiss. The tasteful climax turning heads in the little venue, in admiration and respect for a kiss well done. They had witnessed a sublime demonstration of an upstanding man taking control of a fine woman and giving her what she was partly made for, unselfconsciously.

'Shit Gabe, what am I going to do without you, sweet angel?',

Seraphina said out loud, driving his truck tearfully back to her ranch world in the romantic Texas Hill Country, her medicine, her tourniquet on a life without intimacy. A gorgeous, loving, fit woman alone, yearning, packing the void with activity, powerful activity, driven by her transposed libido. She had noticed of late that whenever she stepped outside of her beautiful Turtle Creek life and mixed with people, she felt her singleness too intensely.

It made her uncomfortable and a feeling of pure grief rose up from the pit of her stomach threatening to reduce her to a painful drop. She pulled herself together and picked up some groceries from Walmart and a new lipstick and nail-polish. She thought she might give herself a long overdue pedicure that evening. She got to thinking about Cricket, he was recovered now and looking sprightly and gleaming, stream-lined without his horns and piratical with one eye missing. He was unsettled of late so Seraphina decided to surprise him and find him a nice little nanny goat and who knows they might even produce a kid or two.

'Fresh goats' milk, umm I could make yoghurt and cheese,' Seraphina imagined, so off she went in search of new and extra livestock. She'd picked up a copy of the Droversville Times and flicked through the classified ads, soon finding just the one she was looking for.
'Free nanny-goat to good home', the advert gave an address and said, 'No need to telephone, just come on by.' So Seraphina headed off to Medina and was there in forty minutes. A pleasant, flat green part of the world, quite different from where she lived, a different aura altogether. She found the dirt track leading to her destination easily and bumped along up to the house. The only sound was the jingling and chiming of bells dangling from the free-range goats. Stepping out of the truck they all came gambolling towards her at a hundred miles an hour. Pure mischief and hilarious riotous behaviour. Jumping in the truck through the open door, pouncing on the groceries in the back and trying to remove Seraphina's clothes. She laughed so much that she could hardly speak and it did her good. Eventually a terribly nice lady materialised and had to bend down and dig Seraphina out of the of the pile of mad, jumping goats.
'Hello, I'm Seraphina and have a good home to offer to a little nanny goat, for my billy goat Cricket.'
'Great, I'm Lavinia and you can more or less take your pick.'

Lavinia was a high-powered New Yorker, charming and direct. As well as her goats she had an incurable passion for Peruvian Gaited ponies, and immediately introduced them to her grateful visitor. Carried away with the wonder of her special horses, they forgot about the nanny goat and went riding. The sensation was out of this world to Seraphina. The Peruvian Gaited pony was a dainty little creature with an exquisite dish nose, and bred with a very special feature that allows the smoothest ride known to man. Any horse's leg is a stupendous piece of natural engineering but a 'gaited' horse has a built-in shock-absorber, as the heel drops down lower than other breeds, making a soft spring in every single step. The rider sits still in the saddle like a light angel sweeping by on a soft cumulous cloud. Lavinia had chosen Medina for the unusually flat land, to take full advantage of the sensation of riding her cherished breed.

'Well Lavinia, I can honestly say that was out of this world. Thanks so much, I'm blown away actually.'

'It was a pleasure and don't forget I breed these babies, so if you fancy one just let me know.'

Seraphina was anxious to get back to her ranch, it was getting late and she was tired out. So with the sweetest, long-lashed nanny goat tied into the seat behind her, she set off. The goat had a perfect round tummy and when Seraphina had mentioned this to Lavinia she laughed. 'I know, two for the price of one .. She's about ready to drop her first kid.'

Lavinia had chatted a lot when they were riding and mentioned the narrow escape her valuable Peruvian Gaited mares had survived, when 'two massive mules from nowhere', had thundered into her barn and wreaked havoc. It was only when driving home that Seraphina gasped out loud, 'Oh My God .. those were my mules, bloody Betsy and Leopold!'

It was late afternoon when she reached the ranch and was glad to be back in the familiar landscape. She hopped out of the truck and trotted down to Cricket, cooing the wonderful news and moving him into the round pen. Next, she fetched a swatch of hay, a useful distraction when introducing new livestock to others and led the little pregnant nanny-goat out of the truck and through the floral meadow where Cricket was waiting. Well, Cricket was beside himself with glee, and the two goats bleated furiously to each other and ran round and round the round pen rubbing shoulders and falling over in tumbling dizzy spells, this went on for a good hour. Thirsty and tired they lay down next to the untouched hay and fell asleep leaning affectionately on one another, Cricket and Mirabelle, a match made in Heaven.

'Well I'll be damned!', shouted E.B., skidding to a halt on Thunder, her lovely black horse.

'Hey E.B., you never guess what I rode today ..'

'Please tell me it was a man, Miss Miraculous, tell me it was a man.'
'Very funny I'm sure,' laughed Seraphina. 'No, it was a Peruvian Gaited pony over in Medina.'
'How was it?'
'Awesome, like being on a hovercraft.'
'Well I guess that's better 'an nothin.'
'Anyway, Cricket's got a wife, meet Mirabelle.'
'Yup, makes you kinda envious seeing all that meaningful affection between a couple of old goats.'
The two of them were laughing now, as they always did, one out-joking the other and creasing up at their own humour.
It bothered E.B. that Seraphina was blinkered to the idea of a real live man in her life and that Miss Miraculous was getting older when she could be getting younger. E.B. didn't care a fig about appearances but where Seraphina was concerned she did. Miss Miraculous was a catch she had guts. 'Man oh man, what a waste of a good woman' E.B. would mutter to herself whenever she got to thinking about it.
Seraphina was not cynical about men, she knew that wonderful individual beings called men were out there, Tall Jake was a prime example. Yet she lived her life like a happy loyal wife never flirting when mixing with men outside of the one she was married to, except she wasn't married, she didn't even have a boyfriend.
There sometimes comes a point in a woman's life, usually when she's a bit older and a little

battle-scarred, when she wakes up one morning and says, 'Right that's it. Enough is enough ok? I'm going to stop feeling earnest and guilty and live my life the way I want to live it. The way which makes me feel spot-on and complete.' It's an instinctive response to living a worthy life, not seeking a reward, then finding oneself in the quagmire of 'looking back', of 'hindsight', of 'if only'. Seraphina was almost reaching that point but wasn't quite there yet. In her case it was going to take something cataclysmic, to snap her out of living alone with the ghost of a dead cowboy named Gabe.

Now, Jake had fallen in love with Seraphina the day he set eyes on her. The day she was spattered with blood from hacking away at Bill's and Ben's ears, the day she stood on the back porch in her floury apron over her blood-spattered chaps and vintage spurs, offering mouthwatering Cakes of Wales. Jake was a real catch, a jewel of a man and a perfect match for Miss Miraculous, if she only but knew, if she would only open her big blue eyes and give in, surrender. Gabe was the old Texas and Jake was the new Texas. Like Seraphina he was educated, and had a passion for books as well as a real deep-rooted love of the land and the people. He looked out for the smaller outfits and looked after his own land as a preservation vocation not a profit-making ranch. His privileged start in life equipped him for the modern world, where big bucks needed to be made elsewhere to sustain an old and cherished way of life. As Jake reticently put it, he'd 'done well in business.'

Deep in the heart of The Hill Country was his famous historic spread called Twine Ranch. It covered square miles, not acres, and had been in Jake's family since the mid-nineteenth century. Back then the family settled the land and took the risk of living in isolation surrounded by Comanche, fierce and plentiful. It was another two decades or more before the last skirmish with these Indians was fought.

The Ranch was out of this world with every kind of terrain and sample of the land's variance. Hills and springs and meadows and steep high bluffs, and divine valleys and long flat plains smashing into vertical canyons, a beautiful rugged part of Earth, inhabited by plentiful wildlife drinking from crystal clear rivers and lakes. Every single vista and view on Twine Ranch was breathtaking. A Paradise on Earth. Jake was in his early-forties and it was his Uncle Davey who had died three years into a happy wonderful marriage to E.B, leaving her a widow. Jake knew all about living with ghosts, he'd been widowed at twenty-nine with three boys under the age of six. The kids were grown up now and Jake had done a wonderful job of bringing them up alone.

'Come on E.B., quit hassling me about real men. Give me a ghost any day.'

Seraphina felt the need for speed and was expertly throwing a saddle on Storm, a horse to die for and fast as hell.

'Well, your looks ain't gonna last forever you know. Then what? To late that's what.'

Astride Storm now and spinning all over the place, Seraphina made a final check on the tightness of the cinch and with a glint in her eye said, 'Right, that's it! Last one to Crack Knee Hill is a ninny!' Boy oh boy those two horses took off like jump-jets before digging deep and smoothing out to a Yahoo gallop. E.B. and Seraphina laughing and Storm and Thunder zig-zagging the pot-holes and straight into the creek. A right-angle turn in deep water heading down stream and out over the green bank and away. They were both carrying loaded rifles and feeling carefree. A nod to each other was enough of a signal at that speed to pull out the guns, aim and fire.

'Windage and Elevation, Miss Miraculous. Windage and Elevation'

tutored E.B.

'Yes Mam.'

They reached Crack Knee Hill and inspected the straight row of trees crowning it, their target. They had a strike, E.B.'s scoring dead centre and Seraphina's nowhere to be seen.

'You gotta learn to float when you're squeezing the trigger'

'Yes Mam.'

E.B. headed on to her place, shaking her head and chuckling to herself and Seraphina headed back to hers, giving Storm his head on a loose rein and just enjoying the beautiful soft evening sunset. Horse and rider puffed out and smiling with endorphins, elated.

Before going to bed that night Seraphina had a hot bath and paid some attention to her feet. An hour later she was asleep with pink painted toenails.

Chapter Thirteen

'Right then you two, let's get smartened up .. We've got guests this evening'. It was a gorgeous day and Seraphina was looking forward to taking her new Tierra Cindy friends for the promised sunset hay-ride in the mule wagon. Leopold and Betsy were surprised to find they were actually required, having got used to being big pets since the arrival of their new owner. Leopold had never been bathed before, and before he could say 'Eee Haw' he was having a good scrubbing with a brush and bubbles. Betsy liked the soapy bubbles and amused herself eating them off Leopold. They were like two lumpy sticks of candy-floss and Seraphina led them over to the tap and hosed them in clear water. Then she walked them, gleaming and tied them at the hitching post to dry off in the sunshine. Next, she dragged all the heavy harness and tack out of the barn and onto the grass, where she'd laid out a big sheet. Two hours later she'd finished cleaning the dusty gear and it was worth all the effort. The big old wooden wagon weighed a ton and could only be manoeuvred with the harnessed power of two mules, so Seraphina cleaned it out where it rested, in the barn facing the right direction. For extra comfort she put out some cushions and blankets to soften the hard benches which ran along the inside of the open wagon. The massive wooden wheels, rimmed with steel, were polished up with wax and dubbing.

'Well I must say, we should cut quite a dash this evening,' talking to Leopold and Betsy.

After giving both mules a good grooming she oiled their feet and plaited their tails and manes, weaving leaves and flowers into both. They looked just dandy and were enjoying all the attention, obediently allowing themselves to be stabled for further coddling.

'Now you're both going to be using more energy than normal today so I think I'll give you a small feed.'

Betsy and Leopold were astounded when Seraphina gave them oats. Within an hour of digesting, both mules were alert and their

normally waggly ears had stopped lolling and were bolt straight, pointing forward almost like horses and nothing like donkeys.
'Now let's think, can I remember everyone's names for introductions at The Drover tonight? We've got Hellfire and Viper, Scorpion and Ice, Juice and Mixer, Widow and Blue and Chilli One and Chilli Two ... good.. easy.'
Seraphina was pleased she could remember all the names and was looking forward to playing hostess that evening.

The hitching-up process of the mules to a big wagon took some doing, so Seraphina had decided to do it before meeting her guests from Tierra Cindy, so that everything would be ready. It took her more than an hour and she found herself rushing to get to The Drover in time. Betsy and Leopold were as good as gold and stood patiently all hitched up ready for the off. She closed the barn door in case they got any ideas and made sure the wheel brake was on good and tight. Hopping into the truck she headed off to The Drover and was there in ten minutes, in time to pop in and say 'Hi' to the regulars and E.B. This was the first time Seraphina had been inside and she was amazed to find so many people chatting away and having a really great time. The atmosphere was warm and friendly and in no time at all she was offered a beer by Tom the barman. 'Thanks Tom, just the one though because I'm taking some friends out for a sunset hay-ride in the mule wagon and I haven't driven one before.'

Well, you could hear a pin drop, the whole bar went silent with this information followed by shaking shoulders and suppressed laughter.

It was E.B. who tried to act normal by saying, 'Well just remember to lean back when you pull on the reins and keep your elbows in and hands down.'

'Ok thanks E.B. You wouldn't like to come along would you?'

'Umm that's a mighty kind offer but sadly I have to check on a sick cow over at mine so maybe some other time.'

E.B. introduced Seraphina to the regulars. 'This here is Tom who owns the joint and over there is Tall Jake, who you've already met. Jake touched his hat and gave her his lovely deep smile again. Then there's Max and Ruby, Nat and Mabel and this here is my old friend Straight Knee Standing, he's Comanche.'

'Well I'm very pleased to meet you all, this is great.' said Seraphina.

The sound of spinning wheels on gravel turned all heads to the door as a motorcade of brand-new top-of-the-range trucks swept onto the dirt patch outside.

'Hell, are we expecting The President or somethin?' said Mabel with a sideways expression.

‘Oh no, those are my friends coming for the hay-ride.’ Laughed Seraphina.

Efficient slamming of truck doors, followed by what sounded like a platoon marching, had the locals transfixed, waiting with bated breath for what was about to burst through the little crooked door.

‘My oh my ..’ whispered E.B. ‘The Restricted Ones are among us.’

Seraphina’s guests swept into The Drover in what can only be described as full combat gear, the only thing separating them from actual US Special Forces Operatives was their age and the label printed on their baseball caps, which read TIERRA CINDY RANCH instead of US MILITARY. The same logo was also displayed where their pips and medals would have once been.

‘Hi everyone, you made it then?’ said Seraphina.

‘You bet! We’ve been looking forward to this all day!’ shouted Hellfire. Viper and Scorpion were already ordering drinks from Tom and flirting in a gladiatrix manner with glinting teeth and shiny red nails. Tall Jake and Straight Knee Standing were cornered by Widow telling them her old man was Blue, and Juice and Mixer were canoodling at the juke box. When Blue finally materialized from the bathroom, he walked straight over to where his wife was holding forth and said to Straight Knee Standing, ‘Yes, that’s right I’m Blue and mighty pleased to meet you.’

Straight Knee Standing said he was sorry to hear that and hoped the mule-ride would cheer him up.
Chilli One and Chilli Two were enchanted with E.B. and got to talking straight away about Mexico and how they missed living on the big ranch, now they were retired. Ice, Scorpion's husband, chatted away to Ruby and Mabel about religion and politics, the two ladies wondering if they were being secretly filmed for a comical reality show. Max and Nat sidled over to Seraphina and staring at Hellfire's waist asked her, 'Are those hand grenades he's packin'?'
'Good Heavens no, I'm sure they're just water bottles' laughed Seraphina and soon the jolly atmosphere had the whole bar rolling with laughter and slapping their knees and it was still only half past eight.
'Well, we'd better get going for that mule ride or poor old Betsy and Leopold will be getting itchy feet' announced Seraphina and off they went.
'Just follow me, chaps.'
The motorcade swirled up and away towards Turtle Creek Ranch, egged on by the locals, like fans on a campaign trail, some having clambered onto the roof of The Drover just to wave longer.
In no time at all Seraphina had shown her guests onto the back porch overlooking the floral meadow, where they were to wait while she drove the wagon around from the barn to pick them up. Before heading for the barn Seraphina

shouted, 'Someone fetch me the Winchester, I might do some target practice.'
Betsy and Leopold were cool as cucumbers and had their ears pricked forwards, listening to all the unfamiliar voices chatting in the distance. Seraphina opened the double barn door wide, did a final check on the reins and harness and hopped aboard. Steering the wagon out of the barn towards the back porch she became aware immediately that she couldn't stop her oat-fed willful mules, and on the second lap around the house, to a second lot of applause and cheering from the jolly platoon, she shouted instructions as she whizzed by, juddering on the excruciatingly hard wood on which she was being jolted senseless.
'Right then, stand on the porch rail one at a time and when I say jump, just throw yourself into the wagon, ok?' Scorpion and Viper were up first and really enjoying the prospect. 'On the count of three jump – one, two, three – jumpppump.' The two ladies were aboard, rolling around inside the wagon. Next lap it was Hellfire and the Winchester followed by Blue, all in one hit.
'Good. Excellent. Well done you guys.' Shouted Seraphina bouncing like a broken rag doll at the helm of a nightmare. Lap number six saw Ice and Widow hurl themselves off the porch rail with such ferocity that they flew clean over the wagon landing face down in the floral meadow, before gravity and speed had their way and roly-polyed them into the creek. Lap seven took Chilli One and Two without too much trouble except Chilli

Two caught her shirt on a nail under the porch roof and landed in the wagon on all fours, topless. Lap eight took Widow with squelching boots, landing like a beached whale and winding Hellfire. Lap nine was faster now and Ice had managed to grab Seraphina's towelling bathrobe from the house to help him dry off. Dressed like a Major in drag he flew through the air as they all counted 'one, two, three – jumpppp!', and landed safely, a vision in fluffy lilac. The voluminous dressing gown covered Seraphina's face, causing her to fall backwards into the wagon still clutching the reins and trying to act natural.

'Excellent. Right. Everyone sitting comfortably?' Seraphina screamed, over the deafening sound of thundering mule hooves and wood wheels on hard ground. 'Well yeh, in a Ben Hur kinda way.' Shouted Chilli Two, half naked, her shirt blowing in the wind from the porch roof, a long way off now. Blue had turned red seeing his neighbour in a new light in her undergarments. She was wearing a go-to-hell corset in teal and magenta silk and lace, jiggling up and down still on all fours, unable to right herself. Everyone's baseball caps were either on sideways now or missing altogether. 'Holy shit – where's Juice and Mixer?' shouted Seraphina. In all the hubbub they'd been almost forgotten, hanging on for dear life balanced on the little step at the back, only inches from the rushing ground. By the time they were hauled aboard the soles of their boots had been worn clean through and their socks showed. Trying to slow Betsy and Leopold by pulling on the reins was about as effective as trying to stop a steam train with blue-tac. Seraphina had left the cheek pieces supporting the bit in the mouth, too loose, giving the mules the relished chance to clench the bits between their teeth. Betsy and Leopold were in heaven hurtling along at full pelt without a care in their muley world.

'Hang on to your hats folks! I'm going to run some steam out of these babies.' Seraphina pulled out the long whip and used it. CRACK! 'Yee Haaa! Right you bastards! Show me what you've got!' CRACK! went the whip again. What a sight they made, Seraphina riding shot-gun like Boudica on her blade-wheeled chariot, and ten brave individuals holding on with gritted teeth and incredible composure under the circumstances. The wagon was going hell-for-leather and everyone was spattered with white gunk flying back from the frothing mouths of two crazy mules. The sunset was awesome as it flashed by in a nanosecond, distorted by the G-Force. Heading straight for Crack Knee Hill at a break-neck gallop, Seraphina prayed the steep incline would finally slow down proceedings or stop the wagon in its tracks with a head-on collision with the big trees along the top. The mules conked out, mercifully, on the crest of the hill and dawdled to a stop, snorting heavily, and soaked in foaming sweat. Seraphina hopped down and tied them to a tree. 'Well, that certainly blew away a few cobwebs, anyone fancy a

lemonade?' 'Lemonade? Lemonade?', lisped Viper with thinner lips. 'Medical aid more like! Medical Aid! Jesus Christ, Seraphina – I've lost my goddam dentures they flew clean out of my mouth back there.'
'Oh I'm so sorry, sometimes you just have to go with it and conquer the problem laterally. I do hope you're all ok.'
The Restricted Ones clambered down onto terra firma one at a time, looking around in dazed wonder as if they'd survived a plane crash and were seeing the world for the first time in a new fresh light. Chilli Two was wearing the lilac dressing gown for modesty's sake and Ice was completely dry after the wind-tunnel experience.
'Come on, let's walk a little and sit down for some relaxation and take in this marvellous sunset' soothed Seraphina. The guests followed and oohed and aahed at the beautiful, beautiful location which mesmerized the soul and freed the spirit of anxiety and shallow thoughts. The Hill Country had a way of doing that. It was impossible not to be calmed by the sheer multi-dimensional aura of the place. The light, the scent, the texture, the sounds.
Everyone was chatting away now after the stupendous white-knuckle ride they'd all experienced and come through together, bonded survivors. A warm familiarity pervaded the group and included Seraphina. Whatever else happened to any of them in their lives again, they would never forget the sunset mule ride at

Turtle Creek Ranch. 'Man, we're gonna dine out on this story for years to come,' enthused Juice and Mixer, waving their feet in the air so that everyone could take a better look at the soles of their boots. Belly laughs and tears rolling down cheeks made a happy sight on the hill that evening, as Seraphina poured out the lemonade and unwrapped another bonanza batch of delicious Welsh Cakes. Tucking in, the group chatted away and recounted the narrow escapes they'd had at War, and agreed Seraphina's sunset mule ride was up there with the best and most hairy of them. 'Found them' called out Scorpion; she'd gone to look for Viper's dentures amongst the pretty wild flowers and spotted them glinting like a beacon, so brilliant white was the finish. Viper was so relieved and after swilling them in some lemonade, popped them in their proper place, giving a broad perfect grin to a standing ovation and much back-slapping. Replenished by the delicious refreshments and having altered the bridles so that the mules could feel the pressure of the steel bit in their mouths, everyone climbed aboard for a quiet wagon ride round the little ranch. Heading off right into the dusk, Hellfire asked if he could have a go at driving the wagon and mules. 'Sure thing' said Seraphina, 'it will give me a chance to do some target practise with the old Winchester.' It was incredibly relaxing just plodding along in the old creaky wagon, Chilli One taking snapshots of his smiling friends and the wonderful views. Seraphina loaded the Winchester and took aim at a single tree a long way off, the others asking, 'Can I have a go after you?' She cocked the gun and squeezed the trigger. Leopold and Betsy took off in the split second before firing, sending Seraphina flying backwards, legs in the air. The bullet went straight through her toe and the tip of her pointy cowboy boot was blown right off. There was blood spurting all over the place. The mules were on the flat pasture now flying along at a rollicking pace with Hellfire trying with all his might to pull on the reins and stop. It was hopeless, and the retired platoon clicked into professional mode. Out of their innocuous small rucksacks they all carried, came an impressive mix of high-tech communications equipment, like the carpet bag of a futuristic Mary Poppins. Chilli One and Two Googled Earth on a laptop and had exact location co-ordinates in a moment. Blue and Widow extended an aerial antennae and tapped into the frequency they were looking for on a suped up ham-radio. Viper rammed a file of morphine into Seraphina's thigh while Scorpion packed the bleeding wound with field dressings. Juice and Mixer held onto Hellfire and all put their backs into pulling on the reins. The more they pulled, the faster the crazy mules seemed to go. The radio crackled into life and in no time at all Widow was talking to a Five Star General somewhere in Texas. 'We have a man down .. repeat ... we have a man down ..request assistance... Mayday ... Mayday' A voice from nowhere responded quickly, 'Widow is that you?

Well I'll be, how's it going in those Texas Hills?' Blue took over the conversation, 'Phantom, you old rogue, we got a man down out here and need a bird to pick up and drop off at the hospital.' 'You got it – We got some of our boys out training in your neck of the woods, tell me the co-ordinates.' Chilli One gave the spot in Sat. Nav. Speak, emphasizing that the target was moving, that the mules could not be slowed. 'Yee Haa!' shouted Phantom, the Five Star General, down the airwaves. 'Now, I need you to fire off some flares in exactly seven minutes.' 'Will do. This is Blue signing off.'

Hellfire had a waistband of emergency flares and was stripped of them quickly, while still riding shot-gun behind Betsy and Leopold. The seven minutes evaporated and Widow counted down, 'Five, four, three, two, one...' Whoosh, went the flares and lit up the dusky sky. Whoosh, went another and another and another, then like a spinning ghost from nowhere a massive helicopter came into view. Within moments it was flying above the hurtling wagon and galloping mules. The helicopter doors slid open and a winch was lowered with expert accuracy, the pilot signalling and doing his best to stay level over the runaway wagon. Ice and Scorpion had hold of the winch now and hooked the harness round Seraphina's body. She was conscious, but seeing stars after losing so much blood and was in chilled-out giggling shock, after the morphine.

Up she went defying gravity, and floated onto the deck of a real helicopter gun-ship with a great bunch of guys waiting for her, all cheering when she was safely aboard. The immaculate rescue was accomplished and the helicopter banked away to the Accident and Emergency car park in Droversville. Meanwhile, Seraphina's guests were almost blase about their own dangerous predicament and were so chuffed about the mission they'd just accomplished they almost forgot they were still hurtling along at the mercy of runaway mules. 'Right that's it folks! Everyone climb to the front and when I say pull, all pull!' Ten people tugging with all their strength is what it took to finally stop those mules. 'Eureka!', Chilli Two sighed and sat down in a heap panting.

On board the helicopter gunship, Seraphina was chatting away, powered by the morphine and didn't even notice the nice man in a big helmet putting an intravenous drip in her arm or the other stuff they gave her to kick-start a low, low blood pressure and about the time they landed in the hospital car park the pain surfaced.

'Holy Bloody Shit! Ow, ow, ow, ow!' cried Seraphina. 'I wish my Mum was here ... ow, ow, ow.....' , petering out to a quiet simper.

'Thanks boys, that was truly amazing, I'm so grateful' she groaned.' 'We'll be seeing you Mam, Good Luck,' and they climbed aboard and spun up and away, saluting Seraphina as she spontaneously saluted back from her stretcher.

An hour and a half later Seraphina was all

bandaged up and demanding a cab to take her home. The bullet made a flesh wound to the tip of her big toe, and although it would never look the same again she would live without a limp or any other legacy. 'Phew. Thank God for that,' she said to the nice doctor, who had admired her pretty painted toenails, all nine of them. 'Well I guess that's one less to paint from now on, but I'm sad to lose my lovely boot', she chirped. Being driven home in a taxi through town, Seraphina finally got to thinking about the fate of her guests and even the fiendish mules. 'Oh my goodness, I hope they're all ok,' she said to herself.

The taxi driver began saying something to her in his rear-view mirror, 'I'm sorry, I was miles away, say again?' 'There's a big hold-up on the road to your place, so this might take a little longer than expected.' 'Oh, never mind I'm in no real hurry,' she answered absent-mindedly. The taxi driver tried his luck and drove on parts of the road he wasn't supposed to in an effort to get his injured customer home quickly. Seraphina gazed out of the car window to take a closer look at what seemed to be blocking the traffic. There, almost alongside the taxi now, was a procession, in the dark an unforgettable procession. Sitting at the front of the wagon, holding the reins, was Chilli Two in Seraphina's fluffy lilac dressing gown, wearing a cavers headlamp. On foot, flanking Betsy and Leopold and holding the mules' heads with a vice-like grip, were Blue and Juice, holding torches. Viper, Scorpion and Mixer were sitting in the wagon wrapped in blankets, chatting away and occasionally making wisecracks to the fascinated motorists crawling in the jam. Hellfire and Chilli One were bringing up the rear, and Widow was polishing off the last of Seraphina's Welsh Cakes saying, 'Boy oh boy – am I hungry.' Sliding down in the seat of her taxi, Seraphina drifted past without attracting attention.

The taxi driver muttered something like, 'Man, those Unrestricted Ones think they own the goddam road', shaking his head and looking for agreement from his passenger. 'Yup, they're a real menace, ain't that the truth,' burbled Seraphina. A last glance back at her life-saving friends filled her with pride and admiration. Ice was smooching a slow waltz with his lovely wife Scorpion in the center of the old wood wagon, to the tune on a police car radio.

Chapter Fourteen

Back at the ranch Seraphina hobbled into the house to fetch some money to pay the cab driver.

'When you pass the mule train on your way back, can you give them a message for me?'

'Yup sure, you know those people?'

'Just tell them Seraphina's home safe, and waiting with chilli and corn bread and some ice-cold beer.'

'Yes Mam,' said the taxi man and drove off into the pitch dark.

In the little kitchen, Seraphina hopped around lighting all the lamps. She took a clean tablecloth and laid out a lovely inviting table on the pretty front porch. She heated up the chilli and home-baked corn bread she'd prepared earlier, then dragged a cool refreshing case of beers out of the creek unhooking Chillie Twos' blouse, still caught up on the nail under the porch roof, as she went. Hopping around was tricky but not impossible and she managed pretty well.

The news had spread like wildfire round Droversville, so it was no surprise when E.B. rolled up in her truck and just shook her head at Seraphina. 'Miss Miraculous, the whole town's talking about you and a helicopter and a gunshot wound.'

'Oh E.B. what a night.'

'I'm guessing by the size of that bandage you're wearing, that the story is true.'

'Yup' E.B placed her hand on her friend's shoulder and just shook her head before accepting Seraphina's invitation to her late-supper-come-dawn meal on the veranda.

It wasn't long before the mules and wagon and the hapless ten creaked into the front yard.

'Thank you so much, guys, what can I say? You are my heroes' said Seraphina fighting back tears and feeling the best emotion in the world, relief. She handed Chillie Two her shirt back.

'Hell, are we glad to see your pretty face all in one piece,' said Viper, hugging Seraphina.

'It's all in a day's work for us you know,' joshed Hellfire looking peaky and tired. All the hugging and leg-pulling was interrupted by a snazzy car whizzing up the little dirt road. Out jumped a reporter from The Droversville Times with a beaming face.

'Front page news that's what this is – Front page news!'

Flash lights went off and pictures were taken of everyone including Betsy and Leopold, who were on their last legs and stiff. The interviews over, E.B. led the mules to the barn and gave them a good rub-down before turning them out into the paddock.

The smell of delicious food lured the shell-shocked band quickly to the table and everyone ate ravenously and drank delicious cold beer and hot coffee and generally unwound.

E. B. was on top form and loving all the detail of the evening's events, knowing it would give a good few nights entertainment at The Drover. Exhausted and sore the guests finally headed back to the controlled world of Tierra Cindy and their longed-for hot baths. Seraphina waved the motorcade off and sat down with E.B. for a night-cap for breakfast. A stiff brandy was all it took to send Seraphina fast asleep in the rocking chair on the porch, just as dawn broke. Half an hour passed and when E.B. was satisfied all was well at Turtle Creek Ranch, she helped Seraphina indoors and onto Gabe's bed where she slept fully clothed and with one boot on.

Seraphina woke and was sad and low and in terrible pain. She had opened her eyes, unable to move. The wonderful pain-killing drugs had worn off and her body and soul felt rock-bottom.

'Oh dear, not good, not good,' she said through clenched teeth and pouring tears. It was about eight o'clock in the morning and the sun was leaking through the closed shutters in her bedroom. Desperate for the bathroom, she tried to get up, every muscle in her body felt like it had been through a mangle. Her stomach muscles were sore and she just couldn't lift her torso to sit up, instead she rolled horizontally onto the timber floor and managed to pull herself onto all fours her injured foot at a twisted angle.

'Christ, not good, not good,' she wept, feeling very alone and miserable. Struggling to her feet she hopped to the bathroom, every hard landing sending awful pain through her foot and leg. Sitting down she needed to pull her one boot off and just couldn't find the strength or helpful angle to do it. Instead she splashed her face and cleaned her teeth and undid the tight ribbon still tying her thick dark hair neatly back. She stared in the little mirror above the sink and could see a pale face with rings under her eyes, softened only by the sunlight leaking in, her Celtic blue eyes were deep and sorrowful. 'Alone, that's what you are. Completely alone, that's the bottom line, girl', she said out loud to herself and watched the tears run down her blank face. Still in yesterday's jeans, stained with hardened blood, she tried one more time to pull her boot off, using the bathroom step to yank and pull the stubborn footwear. Finally she was free and reeling with the physical pain of the effort. She took a big pair of scissors from the bathroom cupboard and cut her jeans off, the bandaged foot unable to squeeze through her narrow slim-hipped Wranglers.

A fresh scented pile of clean laundry was stacked on a chair against the wall in the lean-to bathroom and she pulled her blood-spattered shirt and vest off, noticing the bruises around her ribcage and back and arms. She wondered if the other survivors from yesterday were in the same shape, and worried about them. Her bra was crushing in on her and it was wonderful to tear it off and put on a soft cotton vest instead and a pretty pink shirt which she tied in a knot at the waist. Slipping into soft cotton track-suit pants, it was good to be out of the stiff and not always comfortable garb of a cowgirl. The hospital had sent her home with painkillers to take and an appointment card to return in a couple of days for the dressing to be changed. Hopping around barefoot now, she searched in vain for the needed tablets and collapsed onto a chair in the kitchen, panting and crying with her head in her hands feeling cold and not very well. 'Shit, not good, not good,' she said again and shuddered with a vivid flash-back to the moment when she shot her own foot and the red blood spurted everywhere, 'Idiot! What an idiot!' she scolded herself. Seraphina didn't hear the truck parking at the front of the house, or the footsteps coming round the side of the house, it was the gentle tap at the back door that alerted her. Hopping to unlock the big bolts she opened the door and squinted as the bright, bright sunlight dazzled her. It was Jake.

'Good mornin' Mam, E.B. told me what happened and I'm here to offer any assistance I can.'

'Jake ..' Seraphina passed out into the arms of a wonderful man.

Jake swept Seraphina up safely into his strong arms and carried her tenderly onto the soft cushioned swinging bench on the back porch. Laying her down gently he went into her little house and brought two soft pillows from her unmade bed and arranged them carefully, one under her head and one under her wounded foot. Her hair was soft and scented and feminine and she looked so fragile that Jake was overwhelmed with his need to protect her, to take care of her, to love her and to hold her. He pulled up a chair and took her pulse, her heart rate was quick, too fast for his liking and he touched her brow to feel for heat. Seraphina was burning up and Jake guessed that infection had set in. He needed to get her back to the hospital

and managed to get enough of a signal on his cell phone to catch E.B. over at her place and tell her where he was taking Miss Miraculous.
'Hell, I was just on my way over Jake, good man. I'll meet you at the hospital.'
'Will do, E.B.'

Jake had a sleek truck with soft suspension and air conditioning and everything you would expect from a successful ranch owner. He put the seats down making a space for Seraphina to lie in nurtured comfort. Carrying her in his arms she opened her eyes for a moment and looked straight into his soul. 'Jake I'm not feeling very good ... ' she whispered before drifting off again.
'Don't fret Seraphina, I'm here and taking care of you, angel love.'
Rushing now, Jake had his precious cargo carefully loaded and on the road in a minute, and arrived at the hospital in no time, driving quickly on the familiar route down from The Hills and across town.
Jake had called the hospital on the way down so they were ready and expecting Seraphina. He carried her in his arms for the third time that morning and kept a calm vigil over her all day. By the time E.B. arrived, on her willing black horse, Thunder, because her truck wouldn't start, Seraphina was on an intravenous drip of antibiotics in one arm, a re-hydrating drip in the other and a cocktail of pain-killers in between.

She was just coming round from a general anaesthetic, having had the top half of her big toe on her right foot amputated at the joint.
E.B. was shocked seeing Miss Miraculous looking so tiny and fragile in the big hospital bed. The huge wonderful personality was what made Seraphina invincible, the sedated body was a shadow of the person who lived in it. 'Hell Jake, she gonna be all right?' E.B. whispered, standing over her super-duper neighbour lying like a pale ghost. 'Sure, she's gonna be all right, E.B. This is Miss Miraculous we're talking about.'
She came to, hearing their voices standing over her and opened her eyes to say 'Christ, I'm absolutely bloody starving'
Feeling better now and sitting up in bed, Seraphina did as she was told and ordered lunch from Jake who acted like a waiter with a pocket-book and pencil, making them laugh.
'Right then, I'd like a Double Cheese Big Mac with Extra Large Fries and a Large Chocolate Milkshake and Apple Pie to finish.'
With a final flourish of his pencil, Jake bowed courteously and said, 'Coming right up, Mam, your word is my command.'
In no time at all Seraphina was tucking into a delicious pile of food and E.B. was reading the front page of The Droversville Times out loud, pacing up and down the hospital room with a pretend theatrical delivery. 'Droversville witnessed an act of true heroism yesterday, the like of which has not been seen since the days of our very own Texas Rangers ..' and so it went

on, with a great photo of Betsy and Leopold looking like butter wouldn't melt in their mouths, and another of the Tierra Cindy platoon looking funny, propping up Seraphina who was balancing on her injured foot, still smiling, using the Winchester as a crutch.
Jake had popped back to Seraphina's ranch at his insistence, carrying the 'To do' list she had dictated to him in the hospital, reluctantly because she wasn't used to needing help.

1. Check on Cricket and his wife Mirabelle and move them to smaller enclosed paddock, give water and small swatch of hay, see if Mirabelle is leaking milk, she's about to produce her first kid .. if so, chuck clean straw down in a corner.

2. Lead Leopold and Betsy round the flat meadow and check for lameness after yesterday, pick out feet and feel for any heat in the legs. If so walk in cool creek for twenty minutes then turn out onto bottom pasture, the one before Crack Knee Hill.

3. Check the horses, they're running loose on the big meadow right now, if you can't find them, panic! There should be five and they all respond to their own names : Chaz, Mimi, Storm, Lightning and Red.

4. My pet longhorns amount to eleven now, six old cows, and five little heifers. If you come across Dozer the stray bull run like hell! You'll know if it's him, he's brindle with a beat up old face and a sway back, poor old thing.

5. At the house, turn off the hot-water heater in the lean-to bathroom and put my Winchester back on the chimney breast, cartridges in the kitchen drawer, please. Lock back door and leave through the front, locking it as you go, big old key hanging on little hook above the inside lintel.

6. Last but not least, close the barn after parking the old truck inside, keys in ignition.

7. Help yourself to as many melons and peaches as you can carry, they're in boxes in the cool shed opposite the house.

Jake bowled along whistling and day dreaming about Seraphina and got down to the list of farm chores easily with a spring in his step. Putting the cartridges in the kitchen drawer, as requested, he noticed a large sheet of yellow paper stuck on the wall, entitled 'Diversification options!! Very necessary!!!!'
Intrigued by all the exclamation marks, he read the list out loud,
'Chilli Farming, Yoghurt Making, Cheese Making, Bed and Breakfast, Gentling A Horse The Indian

Way Clinics, Bird Watching Weekends, Nature Walks, Organic Peach Jam – Mass Production, Breaking Horses, Collecting Vintage Cowboy Gear Tutorials, Making Custom Chaps For Bull-Riders Lessons, Training Mules ... Your Friend For Life Lectures.'

'Training mules? I guess she'll be givin' refunds on that one..' said Jake, shaking his head and smiling. There was a pen dangling from a piece of string next to the ideas list on the wall. Jake took up the pen and added one more suggestion, it read: 'Or marry Jake and live happily ever after.'

Seraphina was only going to be away from home for one night so she didn't fight it, she gave in and relaxed, knowing Jake and E.B. would take good care of her ranch and animals in her absence.

As E.B. was leaving the hospital that evening, with the prospect of riding all the way home on Thunder, who was still waiting patiently in the car park, Jake was coming in, to report back to Seraphina.

'Well? Have you asked her yet?' whispered E.B.

'No not yet, d'you think now's a good time?'

'Yup, most definitely yup.'

'OK, I'll give it my best shot. Wish me luck.'

'Good Luck.'

Jake started for the hospital door, then turned back and caught up with E.B. 'E.B… I hitched

Seraphina's old two-horse trailer on the back of the truck and I loaded Thunder, he's munching hay. I'll drive you home ok?'

'Hell Jake, I'm gonna marry you myself at this rate, that's great, thanks.' Jake threw his keys to his favourite Uncle's widow, Aunt E.B., as they raised eyebrows to each other, conspiratorially.

Seraphina was sitting in bed feeling dazed and peculiar and watching television. The local evening news was on with a segment about the Tierra Cindy folk and their heroic rescue mission. It was funny to see them retelling the adventure and enjoying their new fame in the community. Seraphina was gla to see them all looking chipper and ok. Fighting the urge to sleep, Seraphina stayed awake, knowing Jake was coming back.

'Hey you … how you doin?' asked the tall, handsome Texan, because he meant it and wanted to know. 'All the better for seeing you Jake' smiled Seph.

'Everyone's fine back at your place and here's your front door key.' 'Oh thanks, maybe you should hang onto it 'til tomorrow, in case they keep me in.'

'No problem Seraphina, helping you is my pleasure.'

'I'll have to think of something I can do for you in return, when I'm fixed up.'

'Well, I have … something … in mind,' ventured Jake.

Seraphina felt herself getting hot and was sure she was blushing.. 'You do?'
'My eldest son, Jake Jnr. is getting married next weekend at my place, Twine Ranch, and I wondered if you would do me the honour of coming along as my guest? E.B. will be there.'
'I'd be delighted, thank you Jake.'
'Great, that's settled then. Now you get some rest and I'll come by tomorrow.'
Walking out of the hospital Jake was pleased to give E.B. the good news... 'She said yes.'
'Mighty glad to hear it, Jake. Mighty glad.'

Chapter Fifteen

After a long sleep Seraphina woke, it was dawn and she knew where she was, in a hospital, having had half a big toe removed.
Hopping to the window she pulled back the curtains and the Hill Country light poured in, soft and orange and nurturing. Sitting back on the hospital bed she was looking forward to having the drips removed from her arms, she felt squeamish about the sticky tape stuck over whatever apparatus it took to deliver the goods into her veins. She'd had to stretch all the clear tubes to their limit to reach the window and the change in gravity meant that for a minute or two her own blood backed up and the clear plastic lines turned bright red,'Ugh'. Seraphina gingerly

placed her arms in an optimum position and soon the lines were running clear again.
She was struck by how different her life was now, her lifestyle was the one she wanted, the one she had yearned for as far back as she could remember, with her passion for life in the Wild West, she'd made it. Just her and her horses and the God-given landscape. Being in a hospital was slightly discomforting though, because it drew her out of the bubble of life she favoured. So she blinkered herself and tried not to notice the ordinary things, like people wearing suits and working in offices and raving about an episode from a popular soap opera. Seraphina still didn't have a television up at the ranch and she liked it that way. She kept up with the news back in the UK through her weekly letters from Mum, who would often include newspaper articles, cut out and posted along with the letters. Not withstanding nearly blowing her foot off with the Winchester, Seraphina had definitely been living the honeymoon period as a lady rancher and she sensed that the honeymoon was coming to an end and welcomed it. She knew the Summer wouldn't last forever and that soon Fall and then Winter would be upon her and the ranch and all who existed there.
There was the question of making an income from the place, or some other source. There was also the niggling worry in her mind that she was alone as a woman when she would prefer to be partnered up with a loving soulmate. It bothered her that the memory of her lost love Gabe

seemed to completely satisfy her on one level, maybe because it was safe. She found the prospect of getting to know Jake a lot better scared her to death. It would mean letting go of Gabe, her security blanket and opening herself up again for possibly more loss.

A cheerful bossy lady doctor came to see how the patient was doing and to decide if she could go home that day. A nurse removed all the drips and took Seraphina's temperature, which was back to normal. The pain in her foot was hardly noticeable, though the small skin graft they'd taken from her thigh, to reskin the resculpted toe, hurt like hell.

'I would prefer to go home really,' said Seraphina when asked.

'Ok Ms Cody, but I am counting on you to rest for at least five days and to take the antibiotics at the correct intervals. You must keep taking the painkillers for at least a week, they contain the anti-inflammatory which will control excessive swelling. Have I made myself clear?'

'Yup.'

'Good, then I'll see you again in a few days to change the dressing ok?'

'Yup.'

Seraphina knew when she was outranked and this was one of those moments. About an hour later after eating a good hospital breakfast, she was wheeled down to the bandaging room and

given a high-tech dressing to protect the one already there.
'Mam, which colour?' asked a fabulously camp male nurse.
'What have you got?' replied Seraphina. 'Oh, feeling sprightly are we?'
'No not especially, but I need a morale boost.'
'Pink, orange or perhaps green?' exclaimed the nurse.
'Green, please.'
The job was done in a moment and Seraphina was told she could walk on her heel and take a careful shower with the new waterproof wonder-dressing. Next, an industrial size sticking plaster was put over the skin graft on her thigh, by the increasingly outrageous male nurse.
'Okey-dokey Mam, no need to worry about leg-waxing when I get to remove that baby!'
'Thanks so much, I'm so grateful, I shall look forward to it.'
As Seraphina hobbled back to her hospital room, leaning on the arm of the nurse who'd wheeled her there, the lady doctor passed them saying, 'Hell you just lost me ten bucks!' Seraphina was baffled, 'How did I do that?' The nurse laughed.
'Oh you chose green and we all bet on pink.'
'Why would you all bet on pink?'
'Well, you're Miss Miraculous aren't you? The one that carries a gun with bows on right?'

Seraphina had another few hours to kill before they would release her from hospital. Jake had phoned and his Droversville accent was perfectly mesmerizing to her and her heart rate increased on hearing his voice. Sitting in a chair resting her luminous green foot, she opened the window a little and listened to all the voices coming from the town stockyards next door. As well as holding weekly cattle auctions the huge stockyard sheds also made the venue for regular rodeos and bull-riding competitions. Many a life had been saved because of its proximity to the hospital, an injured bull-rider could be popped over the fence and straight into A & E, along with a steady stream of lady barrel racers with cracked ribs, bronc riders with bust collarbones and even the occasional little put-upon heifer, all dislocated round the hips because of some rookie wannabe cowboy pulling too hard on a nervous rope.

The last time Seraphina had been there it was to sell Buttercup and Blossom along with their offspring Bill and Ben and she was still feeling guilty about it. She'd been there once before, when Gabe was alive. He was out of town taking his old Mum to the eye hospital in San Antonio to have her cataracts lasered. Looking for something to fill her evening alone, she'd picked up a local newspaper and decided to go to the advertised bull-riding competition. She hadn't read the advert in detail, so found herself part of something unexpectedly moving, an evening she would never forget. Stepping through the Alice In Wonderland door, dwarfed by the enormous shed, she had entered a hushed world, that evening. The usual sounds of country music and the loud hubbub of excited spectators associated with a bull-riding event were absent. The dangerous bulls were there, the gutsy competitors were there, even the spectators and food vendors were there but the sound was not. The bull-proof steel, round pen arena was all set up and the milling around of horses and bulls had stirred up the red-brown earth underfoot. Illuminated, floating in the air, like a sepia gel on a film camera, it was like stepping into an old photo, in an old pioneer grandma's album. Long trestle tables were set out in rows and people were sitting at them here and there, eating hunks of delicious beef, cooked slowly for days with smoke and mesquite wood. There was no smacking of lips or belching of air, just quiet reverent chewing, no small talk and no glugging of drinks, not even the sound of dropped cutlery was present. A silent muffled courteous aura pervaded everything. The small arena was softly lit, more by accident than intent, which helped enhance the already soft, hushed atmosphere. The sand and dirt being kicked up had made a smoky mist, an ethereal feeling overpowered the event, the 'activity', anything but dreamy, it was tough, brutal, dangerous and fast. A deep Southern drawl crackled over the low-tech P.A. system, a voice that held your attention. 'Ladies and Gentlemen, please welcome our competitors, some of whom have driven for two days round the clock to be here tonight to honour

our friend Samuel R. Blix, Champion, Teacher, Mentor, Hero and all round Legend. We miss him, love him and celebrate his life here tonight this evening.' Instead of clapping and cheering, the spectators remained quiet, not silent exactly, you could hear some shuffling of feet and bits of muffled conversation about the great man. Some people were visibly moved, quietly tearful and some just erect and respectful, like they wanted to make a salute.

Three minutes' silence when nothing happened, the arena empty and the atmosphere pensive, all the spectators watching as if they half expected the ghost of Samuel R. Blix to explode from the metal chute astride a crazed bull, in silent, awesome slow-motion, his body electric, convulsed yet silent, chaps flying, fringes flapping, spurs whizzing, a truly ghostly amazing sight viewed frame by frozen frame.

That memorable night when Seraphina thought the atmosphere couldn't get anymore gripping, it did. The tangible ghostly presence faded just enough for the sound of a hundred chinking 'jinglebobs' on walking spurs, to be heard faintly in the distance, getting gradually louder and louder, then one by one in the hushed arena entered the silent competitors. Young men who had been affected by the great man in some way in some arena in all their collective lives, each brave soul wearing his own individual 'Lucky' leather chaps. What a sight they made, standing in a perfect unchoregraphed arc, allowing their

wonderful, individual outfits, so carefully chosen, to be viewed as works of art. Purple, gold, black and red, tan and white, pink even, glorious pink, not effeminate but masculine, trimmed with silver conchos and contrasting Spanish braids with latigo leg straps in metallic silver hide. Electric blue and white fringes, yellow, trimmed with deep orange scalloped edges. Bronze conchos, copper, nickel every coloured metal shape available. Green and lilac long fringed, short fringed black and glossy, pure white suede with a single belled buckle.
A legend had died, a man loved and respected by those who knew the difference between an ordinary person and a bull-rider. Samuel R. Blix had been an icon to the young and furious up-and-coming bull riders. That evening was a memorial event, organised to launch 'The Samuel R. Blix Memorial Fund'. The money raised to be used wisely, helping old bull-riders to have a dignified retirement at the end of their extraordinary lives. The evening begun with such subdued force went on to explode into one of the most stupendous displays of skill and guts Droversville was ever likely to witness.

****

'Seph..Seph..I've come to take you home.' Jake was gently waking Seraphina as she dozed in the armchair in her hospital room.
'Oh Hi Jake, I'm half asleep, sorry. It must be the tablets they're giving me.' It made Seraphina

tingle all over being called Seph by Jake, and the warmth of hearing her pet name, unspoken since she arrived in Texas, brought her close to tears.
'It's ok sweetheart, E.B.'s cooked something great back at your place, and if I'm invited I'd like to join you both for supper.'
'Sounds perfect Jake, just what the doctors ordered.'
Driving back to the ranch with Jake at the wheel, Seraphina fell fast asleep again, her body shutting down almost, to get on with the job of healing and recovery. When she woke she was parked outside her lovely home and E.B. was just serving supper on the back porch. A tap on the truck window was all the cue she needed to open the door and hop out. Without saying a word, Jake picked her up in his arms and carried her to the swinging bench so she could eat and put her feet up at the same time. The scent of his body, his chest touching her cheek melted Seraphina.
'Miss Miraculous! Am I glad to see you looking almost normal!'
'Not half as glad as I am E.B. Not half as glad as I am!', the two of them laughing as usual, unable to stop. Dinner was a mountain of fresh caught perch from Turtle Creek, and it was delicious, washed down with spicy ginger ale and warm bread. To finish off Jake had brought over a bubbling, juicy, peach cobbler made by his fantastic Mexican cook over at Twine Ranch.
'Well I'm going to shoot myself in the foot more

often if I get fed like this for my trouble,' joshed Seraphina. No one laughed. Instead Jake took her hand and looked her straight in the eyes and said, 'Seph, I don't ever want to hear you joke about guns again, do you understand? If you've got this thing about mounted shooting, that's fine but not until I have taught you properly and until you have proved to me and E.B. that you are safe and mindful of the real danger involved, ok?'

'Yup'

'Good'

Seraphina had been outranked for the second time that day, both times by people who cared about her well-being.

'Sorry, you guys, I'm a complete idiot aren't I?'

'Hell, Seraphina, if you were a complete idiot I'd blow your foot off myself!' joked E.B., trying to lighten the mood. 'Very funny'

The three of them were all laughing now, then Jake made some coffee and together they watched the sun set before Jake and E.B. headed off, leaving Seraphina tucked up in bed, alone, and not as content as usual. Lying there, trying to sleep, Seraphina spoke out loud to Gabe. 'Well sweet man, is this it? Is this the beginning of our real goodbye? Is Jake now the man for me?' she sighed a deep sigh and fell asleep.

Chapter Sixteen

It was the morning of Jake Jnr.'s wedding over at Twine Ranch. Jake's eldest son was twenty-five and getting married to his childhood sweetheart, Amy. Seraphina and E.B. were getting ready, rushing about putting make-up on and curling their hair. The fun of getting prettied up was made more so because neither of them had done such feminine things for a very long time. They cleaned up well and looked much younger than their real ages, with pert slim figures all shown off in the outfits they wore. E.B. looked unrecognizable in a navy dress in shimmering silk with white polka dots and matching cloche hat. She was wearing heels in soft navy kid leather and matching gloves, the whole outfit set off by an exquisite and valuable brooch of diamonds and small round pearls. It was a week to the day since Seraphina had shot herself in the foot and she still hadn't noticed Jake's hand-written addition to her Diversification List on the kitchen wall. To hide the luminous green bandage she had chosen a trouser suit, with her slim waist and hips emphasised by the lovely fitted jacket in pale oatmeal. A pretty necklace circled her tanned neck, and matching ear-rings dangled under her shiny dark hair which had extra waves that day. Looking in the long mirror in E.B.'s bedroom they laughed at the sight of each other wearing glamorous lipstick and mascara.

'Bloody hell E.B., we look almost like normal women.'
'Speak for yourself! There ain't nothing normal about me!' insisted E.B.
Bowling along to Twine Ranch in E.B.'s beat up old pickup, they had the radio on loud and the wedding gifts piled in the back. Twine Ranch was remote and the steep winding drive to get there was spectacular, deep into the heart of the Hill Country, not a soul anywhere. Eventually the imposing gates to the Ranch were reached and they opened as if by magic, revealing a saffron caliche track disappearing into the distance, up hill and down dale, like an orange 'yellow brick road'. It took another ten minutes to reach Jake's house set overlooking the most picturesque valley imaginable. The house was a big beautiful timber frame delight with balconies and verandas and pretty flowers adorning everything. The wonderful hubbub of a pending wedding was in full flow, and guests were milling around nibbling delicious Mexican tapas and drinking sparkling wine, served in delicate old-fashioned champagne glasses. The guests ranged from cowhands to Senators and everyone in between, men, women, children, dogs, horses, waiters, musicians, florists, caterers, the bride's huge extended family of Comanche Indians and Jake Jnr's wonderful brothers and aunties and cousins. They were spotted immediately by Jake, who introduced them to his son. Jake Jnr was tall and handsome like his father, but with brown eyes and thick dark hair. He was so

happy to meet Seraphina, sensing that his father had fallen for her and hoping so much that romance was finally in the air for his fantastic beloved Pa. He gave Seraphina and his Great Aunt E.B. a warm welcoming kiss on each cheek before inviting them to go on up to the big house and meet Amy who was getting ready in her bridal gown. 'Amy is a direct descendant of a Comanche Warrior Chief, White Cloud,' beamed Jake. Seraphina went wide-eyed, could it be the same White Cloud that was part of her Welsh family folklore, the one believed to be watching over them in spirit, as described by her Great Grandfather who had emigrated to America? She downed a glass of champagne and let the wonderful feeling of synchronicity envelop her. 'Oooooh spooky' she whispered to E.B. to whom she'd related the strange story and who was also downing a glass of bubbly looking joyfully at the crowds of happy people. E.B. and Seraphina headed up to the house and wound their way up a soft, carpeted, sweeping staircase. The scent of the lilies wrapped round every balustrade was intense, heady, wonderful. Standing on the landing with a shaft of sunlight powering through the window, was a perfect young woman, pensive and gowned exquisitely. Amy hugged her visitors and joked about being nervous, and Seraphina wiped a rolling tear away and wondered what the future held for the young couple. Amy was clad head-to-toe in almost white deer skin. It was the task of the women in the Comanche tribe to prepare deer hides for a bride, and many hours of tanning and handwork of great skill had been carried out on the delicate hides. A dress designer from San Antonio had taken the material and created a beautiful wedding dress. Native American Indian tradition now combined effortlessly with Twenty First Century style. Fringes and beads embellished the bodice and circled Amy's slender waist, with a tumbling lace veil adorning her thick, dark hair held in place with a garland of wildflowers perfectly perched so prettily.

Jake called up the stairs for Seraphina, and the sound of his voice made her tingle as she turned to rejoin the guests. Jake hated seeing Seraphina struggling to walk on her injured foot and looking apprehensive, so he easily swept her into his arms, gently walked across the lovely lawn and popped her on a soft upholstered armchair under a shady tree, calling a waiter to top up her glass and offer a plate of scrumptious nibbles. 'Oh Jake, this is absolute bliss, thank you.' Without saying a word and there for all to see, Jake bent down and kissed Seraphina for the first time, slowly and passionately, gently holding her trembling hand.
'Don't be afraid Seph, nothing terrible is gonna happen, I promise.'
'I don't know why I'm so nervous today, it's crazy isn't it?'
'Sweet Seph, you're doin' just fine .. ', another gentle kiss and Jake excused himself to tend to

all the guests pouring in. As he walked back across the lawn, Seraphina was overwhelmed by the sight of him. He was incredibly handsome with a rugged, tanned complexion and silken wavey hair which came over his collar. His eyes were grey and his golden silken moustache was an absolute turn on when he kissed her, so tenderly. He was easily six foot three and strong and fit. Broad shoulders and lovely manly hands, capable and nurturing. In his early forties now he had reached that point in manhood, where the gangly wireyness of youth had deepened into an older prime. Her appreciation of Jake was there, but if the truth be known she was struggling – a real deep exhaustion was pushing her close to the edge. Even before she'd shot herself in the foot, she was physically and mentally drained. The fun of Turtle Creek Ranch was being overtaken somewhat by the super human, relentless effort it took to run it. Single handed, alone and getting older, Seraphina was worn out. This chronic tiredness was affecting her frame of mind, some days she found herself feeling sad and couldn't shake it off, the usual remedies not working – she was just too weak to saddle a horse and gallop away the disconsolate feeling.

Twine ranch was a wonderland of inhabited natural beauty, it was almost entirely self-sufficient and self-contained in a free spirit way. It had Texas-size herds of cattle and horses and all the finite infrastructure to sustain the livestock and the people who worked them. Its own blacksmith and spur-maker, resident vet, saddle-maker, cute little nursery school for the wonderful mix of children: Mexican, Native American and Texan. Its own cantina, serving home-cooked food, and kitchen gardens irrigated to produce almost anything delicious. Orchards of peach and apple. A dairy, producing cream, cheese, yoghurt, butter, pasteurised milk, from the herds of cows, sheep and goats. Fresh meat, fresh fish and even an artisan silver jewellery-maker. The traditional business of Twine Ranch was extended in the twenty-first century, by diversifying into 'People Ranching'. Visitors came from far and wide to stay over and learn about the eco-system and fishing, and dude ranching and roping a model bull. They pressed wildflowers and went on live round-ups and cattle-drives. Students made use of the conferencing facilities and did post-grads in Hill Country Life. It even had a small museum displaying a thousand Native American artifacts, and Texas Ranger diaries to be thumbed through in white cotton gloves. The old photograph albums of a lost pioneering world were another highlight. The ranch even had its own church with a cemetery of history, lined up and mapped out with posies of wildflowers. The Gun Room was spectacular, opening into the Library of a thousand interesting out-of-print books. Guests often ate dinner in The Trophy Room where a wall of huge benign buffalo faces looked on, stuffed and gleaming. Corporate Days were catered for, and burnt-out New Yorkers found respite and splendour and got put back together again, ready for another tour in their hard working city life. Jake was at the helm of all this and, like his father before him, he would pass it down to Jake Jnr. and his brothers.

The guests were all making their way to the church, finding seats and shaking hands with old friends and new acquaintances. The lovely bride was waiting with her father out of sight, ready to be walked down the aisle. Seraphina and E.B. were ushered to the groom's side of the church and were looking forward to the sweet ceremony about to unfold. Jake was behind the scenes giving his son a fatherly pep-talk and glowing with pride and emotion.

Seraphina felt a tap on her shoulder, it was a relative of the bride, resplendent in Native American attire – deerhide and feathers and plaited hair. His name was Small Cloud Blowing and he whispered something in her ear. Seraphina told E.B. she'd be back in a minute – the ceremony was a good ten minutes away from starting. She slipped out of the packed church following Small Cloud Blowing, intrigued as to what he could possibly want that couldn't wait until after the wedding. Outside now, he indicated to her to follow him up the little bluff behind the church and look through the big telescope, which had been placed there as a permanent fixture for visitors to take in the amazing bird's eye view of Droversville and

everything in between. 'I know your little ranch at Turtle Creek, Gabe used to take me fishing there when I was a boy, said the enigmatic man.
'That's wonderful,' puzzled Seraphina. 'Did you leave a fire burning at home today?'
'Do you think I should have?', she replied, thinking it was perhaps another interesting custom of the Comanche.
'No, it's just that there's smoke rising from about where your house is.' Seraphina clutched the telescope and searched the unfamiliar view, holding her breath, Small Cloud Blowing steered it in the right direction and the smoke was clear to see.
'Oh my God.. tell E.B. I've borrowed the truck and will be back in an hour.'
'Yes Mam.'
'Don't tell her why, just that I forgot my painkillers for my foot.'
Seraphina abandoned the wedding and limped as fast as she could back to the truck, thankful that E.B. always left the keys in the ignition. She drove quickly, crashing over bumps and smashing back down in a cloud of orange dust, out through Twine Ranch gates and on the windy road home. It felt like an eternity before she finally swerved round the last steep bend. The house was burnt to the ground. Seraphina crumpled in agony '... no ... Gabe ... no .. ' She was frantic and distraught running in and out of the hot smouldering ashes, wringing her hands screaming to God above and hating him. She was weeping and shuddering and calling out for

Gabe, she shook and stumbled and crawled on all fours trying to salvage something, anything that would reconnect her to Gabe, as her lifeline to him dwindled away. Ignoring her now burnt and blistered fingers, she pounced on one surviving complete object half buried in the hot ashes. It was the tin of sweets with a bucking horse on the lid, the tin she'd been given by the Probate Lawyer in Droversville, on that first day when she collected the key to her ranch. Kneeling on the ground, rocking forward and back calling out for Gabe, clutching the stupid tin, Seraphina shouted and shook her fist at God.
'You God!'
The sweet tin slipped from her hand landing upright and open, the bucking horse lid rolling off like a small tin wheel, round and round, before toppling. She shoved her hand into the gritty ashes, and went to hurl the tin through the air. But something stopped her, there was something else inside. She looked closer and pulled out a singed, folded note,
'To Whom It May Concern,
The enclosed message was written by the deceased before he died from his injuries. The note was passed to us with instructions to attach it to his ashes.
Yours respectfully,
Droversville Crematorium.

The smudged remains of Gabe's handwriting were still legible.

'Darlin' Seraphina,

It's time now my love to scatter my ashes at Turtle Creek. I love you angel of mine and miss you baby. X'

Crunched in frozen pain and grief and longing and fear and despair, Seraphina walked like a sad robot to the edge of Turtle Creek, and let go of the ashes, handful by handful, watching Gabe blow away in the wind and float away on the icy spring-fed water. The last handful thrown and instantly regretted, she desperately tried to catch some back, vainly grabbing at the air and plunging her hands into the water to reclaim a grain or two of her dead lover. Sadly and slowly, she hobbled to the barn which was untouched by the fire. She picked up a head collar and her Winchester, which had been relegated to the barn, zipped in its carry-case, since the accident. She walked through the floral meadow and caught Gabe's beloved favourite horse, Lightning. He had hand-reared him from a day old. Their bond was special and Seraphina never rode him, his connection with Gabe was so real that she sensed it and it spooked Lightning every time. She loved the old horse and felt his nervousness at not finding Gabe anymore and it was sad to see. Lightning stood still as she silently climbed onto his back, gushing tears of grief pouring down her face. She had no saddle and no bridle, just the Winchester slung over her shoulder and a big fresh horse in a head collar and single rope. Smacking his rump as hard as she could they took off to nowhere at the speed of light.

Hours had gone by and with the momentum of the wedding sweeping along, it was late afternoon before E.B. and Jake had grasped what might have happened to Seraphina. When the penny dropped and there was no sign of Seraphina returning to the celebration, the colour drained from Jake's face. E.B. was frantically looking through the telescope and talking to Small Cloud Blowing. 'E. B.' Jake yelled, 'We'll take my truck, get in.' They drove fast in anxious silence and could not believe that Seraphina had gone to put out a fire without telling anyone. Finally turning into the ranch, the scene of devastation completely floored them.

'Hell, Jake, this is not good, you know how much this house means to her.'

'Where is she, E.B.?' They both walked through the ashes, calling her name over and over again, before Jake found Gabe's note on the ground by the sweet tin. 'Oh no, E.B., over here' He read the note with disbelief, and knew how Seraphina would be reeling with her discovery. 'Let's try the barn, maybe she's in there.'

'Shit, Jake she's taken the Winchester and Lightning's head collar.'

They ran to Chaz and Storm and saddled them up in under a minute. 'We'll track her and find her before dark, right E.B.?'
'You betcha', quavered E.B. It started to rain, really rain, thunder and lightning rain, all tracks washed away in an instant, as the two riders hurtled onward, praying for some Divine intervention.

Seraphina had galloped wildly away from the ruined ranch for some time before the horse stumbled and sent her flying to the rocky ground. She lay face down in the bucketing rain, sobbing and raging at God while Lightning stood forlornly near by. 'Scatter *my* ashes at Turtle Creek! Not his! You God! I don't want to do this anymore! I can't live anymore! What's the bloody point!?' Crying and squirming she staggered to her feet and stood on the edge of a steep dangerous bluff, arms stretched out like a cross, 'Here I come! I'll save you the trouble, God! Not enough was it? Not enough to take my beloved brother away, in his young-man prime! Not enough to make me watch my mother's grief! My father's grief! My grief! Not enough to take away my beautiful betrothed Gabe?
My one chance of happiness!' Her precarious position on the edge was a shocking sight, blood pouring down her battered face and ripped clothing. 'I am tired of being brave! Tired of getting over the fact that I'll never get over the pain of grieving! I'm done with you, God, and I'm done with life on Earth! Priming me up now are

you?! Giving me the beautiful gift of Jake to steal back when you feel like it! You already have Gabe!' She teetered on the very brink, looking upward, arms still outstretched. 'Burn me to a cinder! Do you understand?! Make sure there is no Resurrection! I don't want it! I'm absolutely bloody worn out – exhausted! Go on, I'm all yours!'

Her precarious position was terrifying and her footing was unsafe on the wet crumbling rocky edge, she was in real danger of dying and even though she seemed to want it something stopped her, something she'd never heard before made her still – she turned to look and knelt to reach and take hold of a tiny premature bleating buffalo calf, motherless on the cold hard ground on top of the bluff. Off balance, she fell backwards taking the calf with her. The cruel world receded, and instead of a hard landing followed by oblivion, she found herself peering through a swirling mist with the sound of Indian drums and chanting pulsing through her head. To her bewilderment, the figures of her long dead Welsh ancestors – Morgan and Huw – appeared, sitting with the Comanche Chief, White Cloud. The Warrior was thanking them for saving his beloved wife and little boy from drowning when the young me were moonlighting from the railroads and earning extra dollars sending logs down river. 'My Spirit will always watch over you and your descendants, your spirits will live in my heart forever.'

Seraphina heard the Chief's words as if she were there, White Cloud then walked towards her and placed his hand on her shoulder, while resting the other on the tiny buffalo calf. He smiled and looked right into her heart, before she passed out.

The pouring rain spattered on her face. Opening her eyes, she was still alive and once more in the twenty-first century and still holding onto the calf. Standing up, she scooped the little animal into her waist and tied him safe with the strap attached to the Winchester rifle sheath. Lightning was still waiting patiently, and Seraphina scrambled up onto his back. 'Come on Lightning. We're going home. Let's go.' They took off, Lightning knowing the right direction instinctively and galloping his heart out. Soon they were almost home, with Seraphina holding on for dear life and trying to keep the buffalo calf warm and living – both of them were soaked and frozen. The floral meadow was in sight and Lightning used his last ounce of strength to get them there before falling with a horrible squeal, and breaking his leg. As she struggled free from his heavy body, she knew it was over for her beloved Gabe's favourite horse. Putting the calf carefully down she tied her jacket tight round it's ears and eyes. Seraphina took up the old Winchester and blew Lightning's brains out. She threw the smoking gun on the ground, scooped up the tiny animal and ran to the barn. Mirabelle was in the stable with her little kid. Grabbing a pail, Seph frantically milked the goat and sipping the warm life-saving liquid from her hand she kissed the fluid into the buffalo calf's mouth and he swallowed. Seraphina kept going until his belly was full. She found a warm blanket tossed in a corner and lit a fire in the old stove at the back of the barn. Drained, she huddled in front of the welcome heat. E.B. and Jake had heard the gunshot and were both galloping back towards the ranch from different directions. They arrived together and found Lightning dead in his tracks, the catastrophic leg injury he'd sustained making them wince at the sight of it in the middle of the floral meadow. They approached the barn and walked in slowly, slowly. Seraphina looked up and smiled, bloodied, with a black eye and grazed chin, her hands all raw blistered burns.

'You been in a fight?' asked E.B. softly.

'Yup'

'Who with?'

'God'

'Who won?'

'He did', she held the buffalo calf out for them to see.

Jake and E.B. stared at the tiny animal cradled in her arms.

'Meet Mr Miracle'

Jake knelt and held her in his arms and E.B. cried with relief, her lovely wedding outfit in tatters. Seraphina went on, 'I've done a terrible thing, I've killed Gabe's horse.'

'Hell, Miss Miraculous, Gabe wanted his horse is all. You done a beautiful thing by sending old Lightning to Heaven. You know a cowboy ain't nothin' without his horse.'

Chapter Seventeen

After a good night's sleep over at E.B.'s, Seraphina was back at her sadly burnt out cabin bright and early, carrying Mr Miracle wherever she went. He now had the benefit of a feeding bottle and teat and seemed very pleased with this, making funny baby mooing noises which had them enchanted. The buffalo calf was incredibly heavy and it was only because he was premature that Seraphina had been able to carry him home from The Hills the day before, so she and E.B. filled a wheelbarrow with straw and wheeled him about in that. Wearing borrowed clothes and with a face covered in bruises and grazes and both hands bandaged, Seraphina looked a sight but was actually feeling calm and relaxed. They'd all concluded that the fire must have been started by Gabes' temporary electricity wiring. Seraphina had mentioned before that sometimes when she switched the water heater on, sparks would spray out of the overhead cables.
Her luminous green bandage was gone and had been replaced early that morning with a bright pink one at the hospital, the lady doctor looking at her patient in disbelief. 'What is it with you lady ranchers? You all think you're invincible!'

'Yup.'
'Hell, I had one in the other day, collar bone bust in three places and all she could think about was her poor old cows waiting to go to auction!'
'Yup.'
Seraphina and the lady doctor laughed a lot that morning, as one repaired the other. The grazes were deep and the black eye awful and as for Seraphina's hands, the doctor was not impressed.
'I'm telling you, Miss Cody, if the infection kicks in again you're gonna be in this hospital for a week. Do I make myself clear?'
'Yup.'
'Good, let's start at the beginning again, shall we? Antibiotics for ten days at regular intervals, like clockwork. Anti-inflammatory for two weeks, like clockwork. Stay out of the dirt and muck on that ranch, keep all the wounds clean and use sterile dressings with hands washed. I want to see you again tomorrow because if that eye of yours keeps on swelling I'm gonna aspirate. Got it?'
'Yup.'
Jake appeared in the doorway carrying Mr Miracle, all cuddled up in a fluffy blanket. He smiled and waved the little bull-calf's tiny cloven hoof at Seraphina. 'Well, I've seen it all now,' said the doctor. 'Um doctor? I don't suppose you could take a quick look at Mr Miracle, I mean just

listen to his chest with your stethoscope? I need to be sure there's no fluid on his tiny lungs, is all.' The tiny curly-furred body was gently unwrapped and placed in front of the lady doctor. She was visibly moved, they all were, he was the sweetest little creature they'd ever set eyes on. He was so young, that the red hair buffaloes are born with, was still a part of his coat, he seemed to glow like a little hot coal. He looked up so trusting as the cold stethoscope was placed on his chest and lay still as he was listened to. Next he had his pulse taken and no one was quite sure what speed a baby buffalo's heart should beat at, so they all agreed that as long as the beats were strong and regular, he must be all right. He was hungry and the lady doctor fed him his bottle, cradled in her maternal arms, like a loving God-parent. 'Well, his suckling reflex is about perfect. See you tomorrow Miss Miraculous.'

It was still raining which was unusual for Texas, the universally-hoped for rain normally petered out in less than half a day. People loved it in that region and didn't wear raincoats unless they were working the cattle. It had rained all night and was still raining that morning, making the ground soft. Back at the ranch Jake was using the small digger to create a burial spot for Lightning. He was to lie where he fell, in the middle of the gorgeous floral meadow, overlooking the country he had roamed so happily. Seraphina had lost all her books in the fire and was trying to remember a beautiful eulogy she'd once read, they were the words of Buffalo Bill Cody at the burial of his life-long beloved horse, Charley.

E.B. came into the warm barn and gave Seraphina the nod. All three of them draped in oil-skins stood over the grave of Gabe's horse in the pouring rain, a garland of dripping wild flowers marking the spot. With choking utterance Seraphina spoke ....

'Brave Lightning, your journeys are over. Here beneath the floral meadow you must rest. Obedient to Gabe's call you are reunited now, for if there is a Heaven and cowboys can enter it, Gabe waits for you at the gate. He loved you as you loved him, dear old Lightning. Goodbye old friend.' Amen

It was too much for all of them so they wept. A lifetime of their collective human pain was released, for the good of them all.

An unfamiliar voice broke the dripping silence, 'Excuse me, I'm looking for a Miss Seraphina Trinity Cody.'

'That's me, what's up?'

'Let 'im loose, boys!'

'Oh Dear Lord in Heaven above ... It's Max ... beautiful Max ... my dog!'

Seraphina's beloved dog, her stunning black and tan intelligent Gordon Setter had finally been reunited with his grieving mistress, and the timing couldn't have been better. Jake and E.B. and Seraphina and Max and little mooing Mr Miracle, decided there'd been enough sadness that day. They clambered into Jake's gorgeous truck and allowed themselves to be carried away to Twine Ranch for some tender loving care and good cooking.

Cricket and Mirabelle were warm and fed and safe in the perfect unscathed barn cooing over their week old kid. Leopold and Betsy were enjoying the rain in the pasture before Crack Knee Hill, with good shelter if they needed it. The horses, Chaz, Storm, Mimi and Red were content in the big pasture with plenty of trees for cover. For the first time in Seraphina's life she 'let go', she 'kicked back' and so did her dear friend E.B. They sang all the way along the Texas Hill Country winding roads to the Paradise on Earth, that was Twine Ranch. Max sang along too, something Gordon Setters are famous for, in case you've never owned one. Mr Miracle gurgled and mooed in a buffalowey way and Jake reached back and Seph took his warm hand and kissed it.

'Lunch is waiting you crazy ranchers!', shouted Jake's wonderful housekeeper, Reina, as they rolled up to the big house. Tumbling out of the truck, Max went bonkers with a million different scents to explore. E.B. still crying, hugged Seraphina and said, 'Hell it's only lunchtime and I could use a drink!' The hug, the physical contact, was all it took to break Seraphina once more that day. 'Hell E.B. I think I need a drink too and I'm on painkillers!' she said, wiping her eyes with the back of her bandaged hand. They laughed and cried and lived that day in the glow of human companionship. None of them were alone that day, no isolated sunset suppers overdosing on the view. They were with the people they were intended for.

Reina was bossy and confident and kinda wonderful. She took one look at Seraphina and called for her son. 'Chuey, Chuey, take this little buffalo calf and guard him with your life, bring him back in an hour so I can feed him. Jake, get these women a drink … they look like they need it!'

Jake looked at Seraphina all busted up and for a moment he didn't know where to start in fixing her again. He was fighting back tears and got down on one knee. 'Seph, I love you with all my heart, and want you to be my wife … what's your favourite drink?'

'Pink bubbly. And, yes, I will gladly be your wife, darling thing of mine'

'Well, this is your lucky day and mine too ..'

Reina was overwhelmed with emotion and sent Chuey, still cradling Mr Miracle, to the cellar where there lay bottles and bottles of Perrier Jouet Vintage Pink Champagne.

E.B. smiled and cheered at the sight of her two beloved friends so happy at last. 'Hell E.B.' said

Seraphina, 'this is the stuff I told you about .. you can drink a whole bottle of it and feel absolutely fine in the morning!' Lunch was a dream, delicious food and glorious wine and telling Seraphina the details of the beautiful wedding ceremony the day before. They ate and drank and talked and Seraphina faded. Jake took her in his arms to a soft bed and kissed her. She opened her eyes and kissed him back.

'I love you Jake, I love you heart, body and soul.' Her face was so bruised and battered, she was in such pain one way and the other. She was not afraid, though. 'Yes, sweet angel,' she whispered, longing for his touch. Jake hardly dared to lean on her beautiful injured body. 'Not until you're all better, sweet Seraphina, my beautiful wife to be, I love you.' Jake stroked her head until she fell asleep, then keeping her warm he tucked a soft blanket all around her, blowing her a kiss as he left the room and quietly closed the door.

It was early evening when Seraphina woke and joined the others sitting in the big comfortable kitchen, the rain still pouring outside. She was introduced to Jake's Foreman and his family, and the Head Wrangler and his family, all of them Comanche and she listened to the story of how it was that so many Comanche Native Americans were such an important and integral part of Twine Ranch.

The last recorded battle with the Indians in that region was in 1873 at Packsaddle Mountain, and the Indians lost. The ones that survived as prisoners faced a bleak future. Jake's family had settled Twine Ranch earlier than other settlers dared, and for decades had actually survived and lived alongside the warring tribes without too much violence. Jake's Great Grandfather was a pragmatist and knew the Indians were doomed, outnumbered and destined for an unjust ending. He couldn't alter their destiny but he could placate them and hope for his survival and so he made efforts and brought them gifts and stuck his neck out. By a miracle it worked and he and the family were never attacked.

The odd barn would get torched and plenty of cattle would get stolen and even his wife's home-baked apple pies would get swiped from the back porch but the children were never kidnapped and the women never violated and the men never murdered with flint arrows. When the last bloody battle was won and the surviving Texas Rangers were rounding up the strays and surrendered warriors and their families, Jake's ancestor prepared a list, persuading the captors to release many of them as needed labour, an essential workforce, on which the future of his ranch operation depended. The captors agreed, many of them glad of the chance to help the brave proud Natives to live on in some way. Comanche and Texans alike had seen too much violence and wanted it to end. Seraphina was intrigued and looked forward one day to finding out more, if she could, about her own family's connection with White Cloud and the story of her cousins, Morgan and Huw. She'd said nothing about her own death defying experience and her 'dream' which seemed to show her being saved by White Cloud, and had revealed his connection to her family, that they had saved his loved ones and were forever bonded, she felt so proud of her distant cousins, and more sure than ever that she belonged in Texas. Betrothed to Jake now, was the icing on the cake for her.

The next morning E.B. and Seraphina headed back to Turtle Creek in a borrowed truck, with Max and Mr Miracle barking and bellowing in the back, leaving Jake to get on with the job of running Twine Ranch. The rain had turned to drizzle and the sky was grey as they reached Droversville and stopped at the Bank. They went shopping for an hour and Seraphina felt much better in new Wranglers and shirt, with shopping bags of other essentials to begin replacing all of her possessions lost in the fire. Thunder and lightning came from nowhere and a deluge of rain dropped from the grey sky, tinged with green and yellow from the flashes. Turtle Creek was swollen and dark, along its whole winding length and the banks at Seraphina's ranch had burst, just below the burnt remains of the house. By the time they got there, every last charred chunk of habitation had been washed clean away.
'Quick E.B., grab the goats!'
'We'll have to put them in the truck!'

Seraphina carried Cricket, and E.B. carried Mirabelle and the kid, the goats bleating loudly and shaking the cold rain off their heads.

Jumping back in the truck, Seraphina and E.B. parked a little way away on higher ground and watched as the flood seeped up to the barn and thankfully ebbed away before ruination of the second building in as many days. When eventually the rain stopped, the sun popped out in easy innocence and the bird song was deafening, like being in a giant aviary. All that remained of the house was one stone chimney stack standing in the glimmering pristine plot.

'Well E.B. the flood was a good thing I guess, it's tidied everything up and washed all the horrible charred remains away'

'Yup, it's lookin' tidy, Miss Miraculous .. It's lookin' tidy.' Laughing and wrestling with the goats on the passenger seat they stepped out and got the binoculars. Scanning the horizon it was a relief to spot the horses and Leopold and Betsy grazing happily and enjoying the extra succulent forage. As they walked down to where the house once stood, a crumbling tumbling sound made them both jump. 'Look out, E.B.!' shouted Seraphina pulling her friend clear of the chimney stack as it came crashing down, revealing a huge steel box, in the pile of rubble. Clutching her chest Seraphina gasped, 'Jesus Christ I don't know if I can stand any more drama today ..' staring transfixed at the box. Opening it and peering in like pirates finding treasure, they pulled back a charred blanket and discovered an amazing array of hand-made tools. Gabe's tools, the ones he'd used and made and honed for the job of building his unique artisan house. Underneath in a smaller steel box were the complete blueprints for every square inch of the project. E.B. patted her friends shaking hand and smiled looking up, 'Thanks Gabe ... that's mighty thoughtful ..'

Then two trucks arrived beeping their horns and flashing their lights at Seph and E.B. 'Hey you guys, we just came over to say how sorry we are about the fire. How are you, Seraphina?' Her Tierra Cindy friends had come straight over when they heard what happened, and she found herself surrounded by support and every kind of offer of help. 'Viper, Scorpion, all of you – it's so great to see you and yes, I'm ok. I'll live to fight another day.. onward and upward ...' They all hugged and Seraphina showed them the plans of the house which had just come crashing down with the chimney. 'Hell, I'm guessing that fella Gabe is sending a clear message from Heaven' said Widow. Seraphina announced that the rebuild was as good as done, now they had Gabe's plans, and that a real project was about to get underway. She had already planned to set the ranch up as a business offering a unique holiday destination and was looking forward to making it a reality. She and Jake had discussed it and he was looking forward to showing her how to restore some of the land by bringing in topsoil and replanting the wild meadows which used to proliferate before overgrazing stripped the ground back to bare rock. Jake was a knowledgeable conservationist and Seraphina was learning all the time. ‘Time for a celebration I think .. Come on everyone, the drinks are on me..’ said Blue, to cheers all round.

‘Hang on a little while, there’s something I need to do,’ said Straight Knee Standing, and with that he sang a lovely haunting chant, whilst waving his hands over the plot where the little house had stood. ‘For good luck, Seraphina,’ he whispered in her ear. ‘Thanks, Straight Knee, that’s perfect.’

Off they headed to The Drover and had the best time, Tom making outrageous cocktails and Nat and Mabel grilling big Texas steaks for everyone. E.B. nudged her friend with her elbow, ‘Well are yer gonna tell ‘em .. tell ‘em the happy news?..’ Seraphina downed a Margarita cocktail and bit into the chunk of lemon which Juice and Mixer had lined up for her. ‘You tell ‘em E.B… Why I’d be …. honoured … and proud … for you to make my announcement’ .. a hiccup was E.B’s cue. Seph’s dear friend hiked her foot up onto the bar and ceremoniously removed her glinting spur. ‘Tom gimme one of those crystal goblets and fill it with champagne’, she shouted over the hubbub. ‘Comin’ right up E.B.. Comin right up’ said Tom. The sparkling wine was poured and E.B. tapped the glass .. the perfect ringing chime of a ladies spur hitting crystal brought the room to order. ‘Ladies and Gentleman, I have an announcement to make …. It is my great pleasure to tell you all that Seraphina Trinity Cody has accepted a proposal of marriage from none other than Jake Buchanan of Twine Ranch .... Yeee Haaa!', The room exploded and Seraphina was almost hugged to death, and it took a while before the room fell silent as all heads turned to the door – a man with a big hat carrying a rifle had walked in. Squinting her eyes Seraphina thought she recognized the man, 'Chester? ... is that you?' Chester the Gun, Gabe's lifelong friend stood before her. Tears poured down Seraphina's face, Chester stepped forward and comforted her. 'Hey Miss Cody, no need for crying. I heard that you were to be married and came by to wish you well. I've known Jake forever and he's one of the finest straightest men I've ever met in my life, Gabe would approve, I know that.'

Poor Seph broke down and cried really cried. Chester took drastic action and fired his rifle in the air.... 'Stop that crying Miss Cody, why I've brought you a present.' He handed her a little Derringer rifle. 'That ole Winchester you use is the wrong rifle for you, this little rifle is perfect for you, I know that because I'm a Gunsmith .. Now Gabe bought it for you and I've restored it, the gun barrel got mashed up when we had the accident. I'm gonna stop on by your place tomorrow and pick up that Winchester of yours and properly align the sights. Heck Miss Cody, you were becomin' a good shot when I knew you an' I'm tired of hearin' that you can't shoot straight . Got it?' Holding the beautiful little rifle

Seraphina had stopped crying and said 'Yup, I've got it. Thank you dear Chester, thank you so much' Walking back out the little crooked door, Chester turned to Seraphina and threw her a small packet. She caught it, 'Now those are ear protectors and if you don't wanna be deaf with a permanent ringing in your old age, I suggest you wear them at all times when firing a gun, got it?', Seph nodded emphatically yes. 'Well I'll be seein' you then and Jake Buchanan is the luckiest man on Earth having you as his betrothed … sweet Seph' Seraphina ran to Chester and kissed his cheek.

****

A month had passed since the 'once in a hundred years' flood and it was September. Seraphina was fit and well, as were all the animals, Mr Miracle growing into a splendid little bull buffalo, Max bounding endlessly and effortlessly over everything and loving his new free spirit life with his mistress. The cattle had produced more delightful offspring courtesy of poor old Dozer, and the goats and mules lived a happy carefree existence. Seraphina was project managing the rebuild of her house and was in her element, running things her way waving the blueprints in the air and keeping a tight ship, much to the amusement of the old-timer craftsmen she had on the payroll.

Her bliss was riding the fence line with Max trotting alongside, she never stopped being moved and restored by the environment she had come to live in. So much had happened since that fateful day when she'd closed her shop for two weeks and taken a ranch holiday in Texas. Less than two years had passed, yet her life was completely turned around, resolved almost. Her love of Jake sustained her heart, her love of the Texas Hill Country sustained her soul, her love of the animals she cared for, kept her sane and pretty and as for E.B. and all her wonderful friends, they brightened each and every day, ensuring both her feet remained firmly planted on the ground. 'Dear Lord, I am truly blessed,' she whispered, turning her horse and walking towards Jake on his. They held hands and leaned out of their saddles to kiss a thousandth kiss before giving the signal to 'Let 'em rip!' Both lovers on their horses flying through the awesome landscape in a world from dreamland.

Chapter Eighteen

The rebuilding of Gabe's house was being held up until the dynamite had been set. The necessary water supply was to be taken from deep beneath the rock, beyond the first aquifer and into the second, a mineral-packed natural spring water, waiting to be released from a thousand feet below into a pretty china jug on a pretty breakfast table. Gabe's borehole to the shallower first aquifer was, like many others in the area drying up, sometimes there'd be water and sometimes not. Seraphina had decided to fork out the cash and improve domestic supplies. The borehole boys turned up and set the underground explosion in the narrow space they'd expertly drilled. Boom! The ground shook and like they said, the 'founds' cracked. The concrete foundations of the little house were all that was left since the fire and now they were fractured and sacrificed for a necessary improvement. Like striking oil for the first time, the excitement of seeing a frothing geyser hurtling skyward was thrilling. 'There she blows!' shouted the professionals, while Seraphina and Max danced under the freezing fresh water until they were soaked through. A moment later the fountain was capped, contained and held back. The digger moved in and crunched up the old founds to broken biscuit before pouring in a swirling, squelching river of fresh concrete.

By tea-time the stone masons were starting to rebuild the two chimney stacks, reclaiming the chiselled chunks of rock used by Gabe for the originals. Seraphina had many great photos of the house so it was easy for the men to perfect the natural angles and wonky parts. Restoration was Seraphina's metier, and as she used to do, back in her shop in Wales, with a beautiful

French table, she dedicated herself to the job and complemented the maker.

Her release from Gabe's ghost was a wonderful thing, a smoother confidence powered her now. Her love for Gabe was resolved and put in a safe place, in her fond and everlasting memory he was an old friend now instead of a lover. She felt no pangs of grief for him, she accepted his death, and a calmer more pragmatic woman had emerged, a person who had been through the mill of human suffering and had come out the other side stronger and easier and accepting of the fact that whatever life threw at her from now on, she'd survive, she'd keep living and learning.

E.B. always said, 'Hell, I ain't met a woman yet worth knowing, who hasn't been over that threshold, through that pain barrier of grief, at least one time in her life.' E.B. had lived alone for decades, after being widowed at twenty-one, only three years into a joyous marriage. Her husband Davey, conscripted into the war in Vietnam was reported 'Missing in action. Presumed dead.', only two weeks into his first Tour. Her cherished husband was Jake's uncle and he and E.B. had lived on Twine Ranch in a delightful house built specially for the newlyweds. After Davey's death, E.B. couldn't bear the memories at Twine Ranch and fled to her own ranch at Turtle Creek, and seldom went back. E.B. had always wanted children and for that reason she had made a disastrous second marriage which was thankfully short lived, the experience leaving her determinedly single, quietly resigned to a lone lady ranchers life with just her memories of the man she loved.

Jake and his family had kept her lovely house in perfect order all those years, making sure it was dusted and polished on the inside and repainted and swept on the outside. They all hoped she'd come home one day and live out her latter years independent but cared for and loved, watched over and protected. Jake broached the subject with E.B. 'Come on E.B., move back to Twine Ranch when Seph and I marry next Spring. Think about it?'

'OK Jake, I'll think about it.' smiled his favourite Aunty, who was actually longing to move back now but pride never allowed her to say so.

Seraphina's relationship with Jake was so right for her, here was a man who protected her, nurtured her, took charge of her vulnerability and celebrated her gutsy independence. The bond that linked them was a complete simple trust combined with a burning passionate desire. The first time they made love it was a month after Lightning's burial. After meeting on horseback that day, as planned and riding like free spirits, Jake had taken a blanket from his saddle bag and laid it out on the soft grass under a huge oak tree. They were alone in the landscape they adored and together, yearning for each other and deeply in love. Lifting her down from her horse he kissed her softly and slipped open the tiny engraved silver buckle fastening the belt of her soft deer skin chaps, before carrying her to the blanket. He undid his shirt easily and kissed her on the ground, his smooth chest leaning on her body. With shimmering hand she touched his warm back muscles and ignited. He unbuttoned her pretty feminine top and gently kissed her beating heart. Seraphina squeezed open the clasps at the top of Jake's thigh, releasing his pelvis from the soft heavy leather chaps he wore. A shuddering breathing was all it took before he was able to reach his gorgeous woman and a searing ecstasy swept Seraphina to tears. 'I love you Jake, I love you beautiful man ... ', he kissed her again and again and again then slipped a diamond ring on her finger. Not an heirloom, for the two of them were overdosed with ghostly connections but an exquisite contemporary cut stone, set in a smooth hunk of glinting platinum. Both lovers longed for intimacy and the touch of their warm hands exploring forgotten skin on their beautiful bodies was pure divine sensation, a quenching of a need so deep and so relevant that it literally engulfed them.

A Spring wedding at Twine Ranch was the best news Seraphina's Mum and Dad could think of. The 'clecs' went round the little Welsh town like wildfire and everyone was pleased for them. It was decided that the longed for visit from her parents would be in time for Thanksgiving, followed by another trip for the Spring wedding. Seraphina couldn't wait for them to come and see her beloved ranch and meet the jolly menagerie and of course Jake and E.B. and everyone else. The rebuild of the house would be completed in a few months, in time for the festivities. There were now four skilled workers following the meticulous blue-prints of the artisan cabin, and it was a labour of love they were enjoying.

E.B. liked bringing lunch out to them while they worked and talked about the old days. Her husband disappeared early on during the Vietnam War and all these years later she still missed him, and felt young when she remembered the happy times they'd once had.

Seraphina and Jake would live together at Twine Ranch when they were married and, in the meantime, Seraphina stayed with E.B. while the house was getting rebuilt, which was great fun for both of them as they enjoyed hilarious suppers with Jake's supply of Perrier Jouet pink bubbly. It was on one of those evenings that the two of them got down to solving a mystery. 'Well E.B., I just don't know what to make of it, I know he goes off towards the top bluff and disappears for hours, but that's about it.'

'Heck Seraphina, I reckon we gonna follow him tomorrow, take the horses and pack a picnic lunch and see what's what.'

They were both staring at Max who was wagging his tail and panting happily with his big tongue lolling out, plastered in dust, he vigorously shook his coat. 'Man oh man .. I ain't seen nothin' like it..'

'Holy Shit E.B… That's not any old dust, that looks like gold dust..'

Max had shaken his silken black and tan coat and a cloud of gold shiny dust flew off him, landing on the white tiled porch. E.B. fetched a dust pan and brush and swept some into a large brown envelope. The two of them examined the contents like Sherlock Holmes on the scrubbed kitchen table with a spot light and magnifying glass. 'Well it looks like gold ..... it is gold ...I think,' wondered Seraphina. 'There's only one way to find out, we'll just make it before closing.' E.B. and Seraphina jumped in the truck and headed into Droversville to Saban's Pawn Shop where they knew old Lew would be able to tell them if it was real gold.

'Yup, definitely absolutely yup.'

'Thanks Lew, we'll be seeing you then,' they both said in a throw-away tone as if envelopes of pure gold dust were the norm. Lew looked at them quizzically. 'I know there's gold in them there hills so don't worry, your secret's safe with me.'

'Okey dokey .. Fingers on lips then..' joked Seraphina, smiling at E.B. and wondering where they could get hold of a book on gold-mining.

'Come on, let's call in at Dreeny's,' said E.B with a glint in her eye. Dreeny's Second Hand Book Store in Droversville was a favourite place of Seraphina's, packed full with wonderful old books about the early days in the Hill Country and all the characters who'd settled there. Memoirs and accounts of children kidnapped by Indians, and true stories of a hundred different life experiences, all of them pure undiluted adventure. 'Hi there, what can I do for you today?' enquired the lovely proprietor, Maisy. 'Oh just browsing thanks – anything on mining for gold?' blurted E.B. 'Mining for gold? Well let's see ... ah yes here it is.' Maisy pulled an old slim volume from the top shelf and blew the dust off as she opened the book and read the title out loud for approval, and a hoped for sale. 'Gold Fever by Tandy Peacock, it's a first edition and a signed copy no less.' Seraphina liked the way it sounded and said, 'Ok we'll take it.'
'I'll just wrap it for you then and that'll be $300.00'
'$300.00?' spluttered E.B. into Seraphina's ear. 'You have to speculate to accumulate E.B., speculate to accumulate' Seph
whispered back. Maisy was giving them a funny look, so Seraphina pulled herself tall and produced her famous wad of $100 bills from its usual spot, stuffed in the waistband of her wranglers and Brighton belt. The money handed over, they stepped out of the store when E.B. darted into another doorway, pulling her hat

down as far as she could, 'What the heck is it E.B.?' said Seph jumping into the doorway too like a fugitive. 'Oh nothing .. just thought I saw a hornet that's all'
'A hornet?.. I don't see a hornet, anyway it's the wrong time of year' E.B. was definitely acting strangely and Seph was puzzled but put it down to the sometimes eccentric way her treasured friend acted. They left for the hills in the old truck, clutching the precious book and glinting all the way home. Back in E.B.'s kitchen they stuck a chicken on to broil, opened some bubbly, and sat down to ponder over Tandy Peacock's book. 'OK, we need shovels and picks and, according to Tandy, not much know-how and only basic skill ... seems pretty straightforward.' E.B. leaned in to take a closer look at the next page. 'Not much skill? Hell, we gotta dig all that rock then haul it to a 'crushing mill' whatever the heck that is..'
'Well, that's just a process to extract the gold, I expect, how hard can it be?' Reading out loud Seraphina went on, 'Listen to what she has to say on the subject of Goldfever from first hand experience ... Goldfever was a terrible thing and them that had it most always came to a sad end. A frothing at the mouth was not uncommon and a crazed expression and carelessness was the usual symptoms of the poor souls lost in the wantonness that is Goldfever', gosh that's horrible' grimaced Seraphina. 'They probably just all had rabies' joked E.B.

'Hey, E.B., it says here that real gold in its raw state doesn't twinkle or glint at all, that only Fools Gold does that.' Waving the brown envelope of dust in the air E.B. said, 'This ain't Fools Gold …we just showed Lew – he said it was the real thing.' Seraphina stood up. 'Down the hatch, E.B. and let's drink to Max whose going to show us the way' They both took a slurp of wine, 'The way to what though ... all we have is gold dust and not the faintest idea where it came from ..'
'Oh well whatever happens a picnic lunch out with the horses and Max will do us both good tomorrow.'

Next day they saddled up Thunder and Mimi the now unrearing horse. What a joy the mare had become since the smashed egg therapy and Seraphina loved riding her. They took saddlebags each, with a good lunch packed and dog treats for Max, who was leaping all over the place ready for his outing.
'Right then let's get going, we're burnin' daylight' called Seraphina, and off they went on the hunt for gold, eagerly waiting for Max to show them the way. As if he knew, he messed about, jumping and dancing and not heading towards his favourite runaway spot. 'Very funny, Max .. Go on boy, fetch the gold.. fetch!' E.B. shook her head and decided it was as good a time as any

to dismount and take some refreshment in the stunning spot. They were on the fence line between their two ranches and looking straight at a tall bluff in grey rock sparkling in the Autumn sun. Within a moment of dismounting and turning their backs on Max he was gone, vanished. They didn't bother and ate lunch and drank elderberry cordial and chatted about Twine Ranch, E.B. describing the wonderful riding country they were both going to call home the following Spring. She talked about halcyon days swimming in the spring-fed lakes and rivers, hunting deer and singing round the campfire under the stars and about all the companionship of living in a special world and trusted small community. Plenty of space and plenty of work and no such thing as small-talk. 'Oh Lord, E.B., sounds like bliss.'
'Yup, Miss Miraculous, bliss it most definitely is.' E.B. was overcome with emotion and the dear friends hugged each other and Seraphina hoped inside that E.B. was going to find a new soul mate, as she had done. They'd talked about Davey and how tough it had been for E.B. not knowing what had happened to him, not knowing how he had died. She'd gone on to describe how hard it had been to remarry however briefly, and the terrible sense of having betrayed Davey by doing so. 'E.B., Davey of all people would have wanted you to try for happiness again.', 'I know, it was the last thing he said to me before he left for Vietnam, I love him so much and my old heart is still broken.' Suddenly E.B. stood up looking over her shoulder and pulling her hat down

again. 'E.B. what's going on? You seem nervous.. like you're hiding from someone' E.B. sighed, 'Well the thing is I think I'm being stalked … It's a women, not from around here and she's always dressed in a tan trench coat and flat shoes, a round middle-aged woman, it's the oddest thing, and it's unnerving me.'

Seph felt a rush of panic, worried that E.B. might be losing her marbles. She quickly dismissed that thought and reassured her friend that if she was being stalked that she and Jake would get to the bottom of it, and find out who this stranger was, E.B. smiled and made noises to the effect that it was all probably just coincidence that she was aware of this innocuous looking woman following her sometimes when she was in town. E. B. changed the subject quickly saying, 'Well come on we'd better track down Max and his gold' They both laughed at the ridiculousness of what they were about to do. They left the horses hitched to the fence rails and walked the last stretch scanning all around for Max.

Eventually Seraphina spotted his tail wagging out from a small opening at the foot of the bluff. She and E.B. tip-toed forward not saying a word, creeping closer to solving the gold dust mystery. But then they hit the deck, as they definitely heard someone talking to Max. Moving closer, they strained to listen, the hair on the backs of their necks standing on end at what they were hearing.

'Well my friend, looks like I'll just have to try harder this next time. You'd have thought that burning her house down would have sent her sellin' up and packing but darn me she's rebuilding the place ... tonight's the night'

'Tonight's the night?' mouthed Seraphina to E.B.

E.B. indicated to stay still and quiet, wanting to get a good look at the face of a real live villain. The man squeezed himself out of the opening where Max was wagging his tail, and stood up dusting himself off. He was well dressed in a grey suit and tie, and next thing they knew he hopped on a little golf cart which had been parked out of sight behind a large rock, and bumped off and away towards the small tarmac route a couple of miles north. E.B. didn't get a close enough look to recognise him but Seraphina felt there was something familiar about the way he spoke and even the shape of his back and shoulders as he hurried away. When they were sure the coast was clear, they sprinted over to the opening in the rock into which Max had now happily disappeared. Squeezing in as fast as they could, they found themselves in a tiny cave with Max enjoying the remains of a lunchtime sandwich left behind by the man. A Tilley lamp, still hot, hung from a ledge and Seraphina picked up the box of matches alongside and re-lit it.

She sniffed the air with a thoughtful look. 'Paco Raban, I'd recognise it anywhere, my brother-in-law's favourite aftershave. The only time I've

smelled it since I left Wales was at the Probate Lawyer's office in town'
E.B. was bowled over but not entirely surprised. 'Those Probate lawyers rooted through all Gabe's personal belongings, after he died. I remember one of them acting shifty, messing around with that book Gabe bought you as a Christmas present. It was Chester the Gun who had them Fed-Ex it to you in Wales, he said Gabe asked him to, just before he died, that it was real important that you receive it.' Seraphina was staring down a dark hole in the rock into which Max had vanished. He returned in a second, covered in gold dust and carrying in his mouth the remains of an old sack-cloth bag which he dumped at their feet. The dusty, torn bag was still half full of pure gold dust. 'This stuff has already been mined and bagged up'
'You're right, we're definitely not looking at a seam here, we're staring at a big ole stash' grinned E.B.
The precious book, The Cowboy At Work – All About His Job And How He Does It by Fay E. Ward was saved from the fire because Seraphina always kept it on the passenger seat of Gabe's truck like a lucky charm, and right now it was safe in the glove compartment. 'E.B., I've still got that old book, I think we need to take a closer look at it.'
'Knowing Gabe, there's gonna be some kinda clue in there and he sent it to you with that in mind' conjectured E.B.

'There's no time to lose – that lawyer sounded like he might be planning some mischief this very night.' They put Max on a lead then walked back to the horses and headed home.

Back at the ranch, Seraphina pulled the book out of the truck and she and E.B. studied every page of it looking for information, a clue, a cryptic message. Nothing. Sitting on the sweet-smelling bales of meadow hay in the quiet barn they pondered, the only sound was Seraphina tapping her fingers on the closed book and lo and behold she felt something under the plastic cover protecting the original dust cover. She carefully extracted a folded paper, old and interesting looking. There was writing on one side and a map on the other, it read:

'To Whomsoever finds this letter, my gold is yours to use wisely. I ain't got no kin so God Bless whoever I am leavin' this to. Remember me and if my body is found bury me atop Crack Knee Hill so I can look out over God's Country for all eternity. This map is the best I can do with the time allowed, them white renegades is torchin' my cabin and I'm gonna make a run for it. They'll never find my gold which I guess is what they came for. Farewell my
wonderful world I'll miss you I know. Signed this awful day, April 4th 1872 by myself Theobald Luke Cutter.'

‘1872? Oh my God how amazing’ Seraphina handed the map to E.B. ‘You know what? This map is impossible to follow, it would send anyone in the wrong direction so I’m guessing Gabe never found the spot and now we have. I reckon ole Cutter struck gold big, in California maybe, and brought his haul here for safe-keeping and to start a new life, ranching or some such.’

‘E.B., how the hell are we going to get all that gold out of that hole? It’s solid rock on top.’

‘Cutter chose a good hidin’ place, that’s for sure. I’m guessing he lowered down on ropes all the bags of nuggets and gold dust ready to haul up as and when he needed it. Then he got killed off by those renegades and over the years the ropes and sacks rotted away and the gold’s just been sitting there.’

Years before when Gabe bought the 350 acres at Turtle Creek he had always known that some day he would build a house there, right next to the huge old oak tree on the crest of the floral meadow. Now Gabe was a great tree climber and on their meandering trips across The Hill Country it had always amazed Seraphina how he could get to the top in a moment and look out for a sense of direction - they were never lost for long.

Aged seventeen, Gabe had climbed that particular tree to survey the land he’d made a down payment on, and had discovered an old, rotting saddle-bag stuffed in a hollow in the tree. Inside, safely stashed in a tin, he'd found the letter and map hidden all those years before. But the gold had always eluded him. The directions on the map were not easy to follow, probably because of poor Theobald 's plight when he tried to write them down. In a desperate attempt to run for his life and knowing he was about to be caught, Theobald had hurled the bag as high and as forcefully as he could up into the April leaved oak tree, a perfect hiding spot, and if it hadn't been for Gabe it most probably would never have been discovered. Of all the trees in all the world Gabe picked that one, and that lovely thing described as synchronicity had her way, even the date of Theobald's letter seemed connected – April 4th was Seraphina's birthday.

Chapter Nineteen

Jake was away for a few days, having flown up to Washington on business. He hated leaving Seraphina. They were looking forward to the following weekend which Jake had organized. He wanted to show her round San Antonio and they were booked into a gorgeous hotel across from The Alamo, preserved and still standing, and still drawing visitors from all over the world. They were to choose their wedding rings that weekend and to romance and to wine and dine in secluded sophistication. Seraphina tingled all over at the thought of their lovely weekend ahead and longed for Jake and his kisses and his reassuring presence and the way that he loved her and protected her. 'Oh Jake ... I do love you beautiful man ..' she sighed to herself, just daydreaming about him.

E.B. and Seraphina were focused on the job in hand, however, and got on with it, with gusto. Being in love, truly, madly, deeply in love was giving Seraphina an enhanced invincibility, walking on air, fabulously distracted, she reacted calmly and smiling to the fact that someone had deliberately burnt her house down and was after her to do more damage that very night. Even the prospect of striking gold was simply an added amusement to her already, heady feeling of joy.

'What we need is a Pow Wow this very afternoon at The Drover I'll round up my lot and you round up yours.'

'Good thinking, E.B.' said Seraphina and she headed off to Tierra Cindy Ranch for back-up.

They had a good plan. By the time everyone arrived at The Drover it was around four o'clock and all who were present had to be let in on the secret and the discovery that the fire had in fact been an arson attack with the ulterior motive of driving Seraphina to sell her land so that Mr Peterson could buy it and claim the gold. He couldn't just steal it, because it was stuck in the hole in the solid rock. It was going to need carefully orchestrated dynamiting to widen the hole and retrieve the gold. Scoundrelly Mr Peterson had found out about the gold by prying into Gabe's personal effects. When he discovered an old note-book of Gabe's referring to his hunt for Cutter's gold and ruling out all the various trails taken from the map, Mr Peterson had calculated that the only place Gabe hadn't searched was the tall bluff. With the help of a friend who was a qualified surveyor, Mr Peterson was able to try a million different computer-generated co-ordinates derived from the old map and, after a dozen dead ends, he found what he was looking for and had located the whereabouts of Theobald Cutter's hoard.

Some of the old timers summoned to The Drover by E.B. had heard the legend of Cutter's Gold since they were kids. A few of them believed the story was true and others put it down to tall tales. Well, the talk went this way and that and a plan was hatched to catch Mr Peterson red-handed and all agreed that a vigil over at Seraphina's place needed to be kept that night. The reunion of the Restricted Ones and the Unrestricted Ones, who hadn't got together since the fire, was a joy to behold. Hugs all round and japes and back-slapping and E.B. and Seraphina looking on in smiling wonder. The cross section and diversity of personalities and backgrounds was extreme, and there was a warm camaraderie derived from a group of individuals enjoying their differences and celebrating their mixing of different worlds.

Blue took the floor, 'OK then, just to re-cap ... Hellfire, Viper, Ice, Scorpion, you're gonna pitch just behind the barn and wait. Chilli One and Two stay close to the trucks, ready to slam the lights on when I give the signal. Juice and Mixer cover the entrance to the ranch with flares primed and ready for blast off on Widow's signal, which she'll take from me. That about does it, but remember to stay in contact at all times in the usual way' ordered Blue forcefully.
The Unrestricted Ones, not going to be outdone, looked to E.B. for orders. 'Well umm umm ... everyone stay in the cedar bushes for cover and don't jump out 'til you think it's the right moment' ordered E.B. unconvincingly.
'I tell you what,' took over Seraphina, 'Nat and Mabel stay close to me and we'll perch in the old oak tree keeping a lookout. Max and Ruby can hide in the cool shed along with E.B, there's a great view from there through the cracks in the door and Tom and Straight Knee Standing can crouch behind the water butt. Remember, I don't want to hear anyone whispering Psst. All communication to be done by bird song and owl hoots ...' Seraphina was laughing at her own joke. 'No seriously, just kidding ..' she had to sit down now and wipe the tears from her eyes from her giggling, before E.B. sternly reminded all in the room to be careful and to remember the idea was to catch Mr Peterson red-handed if he came to the ranch to burn anything else down. 'Oh, and don't anyone go killin' him accidentally or

otherwise; capture, that's what we're hankerin' for, capture.' There were approving nods and murmured agreements all round. Tom got serving refreshments and a high time was had by all as they waited for nightfall and the planned stake-out.

Jake had given Seraphina a cell phone before leaving for Washington and she was carrying it around, clipped onto her belt. The phone rang as she was driving back to her ranch ahead of the others, to check on the animals before dark.

'Hey sweet darlin ..'

'Hi honey .. I love you ..'

They talked and kissed on the phone, Jake wanting to be close to her again and feel the warmth of her body and the touch of her hand. She was divinely aware of his desire for her, her heart skipped a beat with all the anticipation of being reunited in a couple of days with the man of her dreams, the man she would marry forever. The conversation was hampered by the poor signal and Jake had something important to tell his wife to be. It was hard to understand what Jake was saying but after three attempts Seraphina finally got the gist of it.

'Are you absolutely sure, Jake? I mean positively one hundred percent sure?' she pressed.

'Yes I am definitely sure, this line is breaking up, not a word to E.B., angel, OK?'

'Not a word, I promise.'

The line went dead and Seraphina was trying to take in what Jake had just told her as she drove to Turtle Creek, she was stunned, 'Well, who would have thought it, I'll be damned.' Turning in to her beautiful little ranch she sat for a moment and drank in the view, the floral meadow just visible in the dusk. Michael and the men had finished working for the day and the half built house stood solid and welcoming, making her smile. Leopold and Betsy were standing in the middle of the house also enjoying the view and pleased with the success of their almost daily feat of escapology, having found yet another way to exit the paddock on the side, this time by pushing the fence down like a pair of elephants. 'You two .. not again.' Seraphina slung some ropes over their big old necks and walked them through the creek and out onto their favourite spot, the flat meadow before Crack Knee Hill. Walking back she detoured to turn the horses out into the big pasture, she didn't want her precious livestock anywhere near the house that night in case there was trouble and more fire. Cricket and Mirabelle and Mitzy the fast-growing kid, were safe enough in the round-pen with a cosy place to sleep, so she gave them hay and left the contented trio to it. Then there was Mr Miracle, gorgeous little Mr Miracle, all perky faced and hungry, still having milk daily but slurping it from a tin bucket now and not a bottle. Mirabelle did a first rate job of supplying enough for everyone and patiently allowed Seraphina to

milk her whenever and wherever. Mr Miracle the buffalo calf was a sight to behold, huge brown eyes and a massive shiny nose and smart little legs and hooves, all new and all muscle, clad in a curly soft brown coat. He was still only a baby and was easy to handle, being super-affectionate with Seraphina his surrogate Mum. They were funny to watch together, Seraphina trotting up and down the paddock with Mr Miracle following behind, the two of them enjoying the game and dodging one another, this way and that. Mr Miracle always won and Seraphina always melted when he had her cornered and delivered slippery hot licks with his black buffalo tongue and his blissful expression of half-closed eyes and amazing eyelashes. 'Oh Mr Miracle, my beloved Mr Miracle ... what a buffalo you are ..'
She made sure he was safe in the small paddock and checked that the small, open sided shelter he slept in had plenty of soft bedding and fresh water. Satisfied, she headed back towards the house.

E.B. was waiting and had Thunder saddled up with a good coiled rope slung over the saddle horn. 'If that nasty man makes a run for it we might be needin' ole Thunder.'
'Good thinking E.B. I've just turned my lot out into the big pasture.'
'Well, if push comes to shove Thunder can carry the both of us'

The two friends laughed at the prospect and sat down by the barn waiting for the fun to begin. Seraphina was deep in thought about what Jake had told her on the phone when E.B. broke the silence,

'Hell, Miss Miraculous! Stop daydreaming about that gorgeous man of yours.'

'E.B., tell me about your husband, Jake's Uncle Davey ..'

'Oh he was a wonderful man, and we were so in love and he was so handsome and made me feel so pretty .... I miss him every single moment of my life .... after all these years I can still feel him near me ... crazy eh?'

'No not crazy, E.B., not crazy …'

'When he was reported missin' in action after just forty-eight hours in Vietnam, my world fell apart ... hell I was young and never believed we'd be parted for long ... I'm glad I'm old now because each day I get closer to seein' him again, if there's a Heaven ... I know he waits for me ..'

Tears rolled down E.B.'s face and for the first time since Seraphina had known her, she crumpled and held her face in her hands.

'Davey, sweet lovin' Davey ... wish I knew what happened to you .. I'm real sorry we never found you.'

Seraphina put her arms round her dear friend's shoulders and shuddered at the painful reminder of grief experienced and the capacity of a human soul to endure pain and suffering and yet live on and keep going.

Dusk was coming down and the others arrived, hiding their trucks in the cedar and taking up the pre-arranged positions. Thunder was tucked safe inside the cool shed with E.B. and Max and Ruby. The Tierra Cindy ten weren't drunk exactly but definitely a bit shiny round the eyes and a bit glinty round the teeth. 'Tom ... Tom ..' Seraphina whispered, peering over the water butt, 'How much have they been drinking at the bar?'

'Not much, don't worry .. now they're retired, they make sure they're never quite drunk and never quite sober, accordin' to Mixer.'

'Quick, get down.' Whispered Straight Knee Standing, both knees bent, huddled behind the water butt. Seraphina ran on tiptoe across to the big oak tree and clambered up to share a branch with Nat and Mabel whose heads were camouflaged in fresh oak leaves and sprigs. Mabel's red slacks gave her away and Nat's check shirt came a close second. The wait in the dark was endless and uncomfortable and punctuated with the occasional sound of Widow hiccupping and Hellfire relieving himself against a tree. The feminine passing of wind by Chilli Two was the last straw and the whole stake-out was jeopardized by a collective corpsing.

Agonised suppressed laughing was barely under control when Nat and Mabel fell out of the oak tree with an almighty crashing and rustling of snapping twigs and creaking branches. Like two huge birds they landed in the pitch dark and

completely lost the plot, hysterical laughter cackling into the night and Blue whispering in falsetto, 'Quiet down!'
Composure regained all round, the vigilantes sat stiller and stiller, listening out for the dastardly Mr Peterson, all of them blissfully unaware of what was about to unfold in the pitch black.
Out of nowhere, like a scene from a sci-fi movie, a massive cold light illuminated the lovely barn and scared the shit out of all of them, a terrifying rumbling and clumsy crunching got closer and closer, unstoppable. Seraphina still in the oak tree was higher up than the others and could see a huge bulldozer was headed right for the barn, intent on flattening it. She shouted, 'Quick, he's going to bulldoze my barn!' and scrambled down. Everyone leapt into action, hearts pounding, flares popping off in all directions, headlamps blatting out on dazzling full-beam, horns blaring, all the gang running towards the barn and risking their lives at the mercy of a crazed driver in a big bulldozer. Mr Peterson was still wearing his grey suit and tie and had a horrible, ghoulish expression on his face, Goldfever had got him and got him bad, the man was possessed. The dozer was unstoppable and Seraphina was frantic to get aboard and somehow turn off the engine. Mr Peterson was singing the American National Anthem to the tune of the James Bond movie Goldfinger, moving his lips in an over-exaggerated warped fashion, terrifying and awful to behold. The massive headlamps on the

monster bull-dozer were blinding and the machine itself was huge and towering and determinedly pushing on and on towards the target. Everyone on the ground, including Seraphina, had resorted to throwing stones at it, like David against Goliath. Mr Peterson was still singing, oblivious, until a stone clonked him on the head, triggering a horrible leering defiance as he peered down on them, nothing like the Bible Story. Survival instincts kicked in and Seraphina and Blue screamed out orders.

'Let him go! Everyone get back! Run away!' The situation was just terrifying, and Mr Peterson was waggling the huge, steel bull-dozer bucket up and down as he kept pushing forward, grinding gears and pulling any old lever. With only a few feet to go before the catastrophic destruction, Thunder came hurtling past, heading straight for danger, with E.B. on his back holding the reins between her teeth and the Winchester in her hands, and speaking through clenched jaw like a mean ventriloquist. 'Yee Haa! C'mon you crazy sonofabitch! Smile!' Squeezing between the barn side and the massive bull-dozer, E.B. and Thunder were in mortal danger, then four deafening gunshots were fired in milliseconds from the Winchester. The first two bullets took out the dazzling headlamps, the third imploded on the glass windscreen of the cab and shattered it into a thousand pieces and the final shot hit the solid steel bucket at the front and ricocheted straight through E.B.'s chest. She dropped like a stone to the ground as Thunder bolted, riderless into the night. The bull-dozer was stopped in its tracks, Mr Peterson crumpled over the controls, sobbing and talking gibberish, with E.B. lying in the dirt an inch away from death. Straight Knee Standing immediately began raising Spirits with an extraordinary Indian chant, standing over his stricken friend. Seraphina used Jake's cellphone to summon an ambulance. Hellfire called The Sherriff, and Viper and Scorpion administered frantic first-aid in the narrow space, too afraid to move the broken, bleeding body of E.B. felled and motionless. Kneeling in the horrible space between life and death, Seraphina could see an awful lot of blood-soaked clothing and it was warm, all over her hands now, as she looked into the eyes of her best friend. 'Hang on in there E.B., you're going to be fine.' 'Davey? Is that you? I'm coming, sweet man ... I'm finally on my way …'

'No no no E.B.! You're not going to Heaven ok?'

'Sweet Seph .... I'm goin' and glad to....'

'You can't! I have something real crucial and important to tell you'

'Don't you fret now, Miss Miraculous ... everything is as it should be ..'

'But Davey's not there!' Seraphina looked up at the sky and said, 'Sorry Jake, I'm going to have to spill the beans ... it just can't wait.'

'He's there all right .... I can see him now, calling to me …'

'No no, E.B. I have something I must tell you, I only found out today, that's why Jake went to Washington .. Davey is alive, he didn't die in Vietnam, he was made a prisoner of war and after his release came home to surprise you .... The day he arrived was the day you remarried ... he fled to Canada and started a new life ..
Oh Lord it's a long story and all he wants to know is if you'll forgive him ... that woman stalking you was a detective paid for by Davey to find out if you were free to marry again and to establish where you were.. Davey loves you E.B. ..Jake went to verify Davey's identity and he called today to say he's bringing him home to you tomorrow.'
'Davey? Alive? Hell Seraphina don't you go lettin' me die now .. d'you hear?'. E.B. slipped into unconsciousness and Seraphina slammed her ear to E.B.'s chest.
'Her heart's beating strong and fast, the bullet must have missed it. Come on, let's get her moved from here and ready for the ambulance, we've got a life to save!'
They all carried E.B. to the ambulance which had just arrived with flashing lights and eerie siren. The paramedics did a fine swift job and Seraphina rode in the back, praying like mad for her friend.
The cell phone rang, it was Jake. Seraphina burst into tears.
'Oh Jake, E.B.'s been shot and was about ready to throw in the towel to join Davey in Heaven so I

had to tell her …' she sobbed over the wailing siren.
'Well, if that doesn't keep her alive nothing will. Telling her was the right thing to do, Uncle Davey is with me now and we're just getting a plane ride and should be home by morning. I love you angel of mine' and the line went dead.

The paramedic was doing his best to keep E.B. alive, her heart had stopped twice while Seraphina was on the phone and all hell had broken loose in the back of the ambulance.
'One Two Three ... Boomph ..', went the electricity into E.B.'s brave heart. It worked and they were just a few minutes from Droversville Hospital.

Chapter Twenty

The next four hours passed in a blur for Seraphina, waiting anxiously. She remembered the sight of seeing E.B. being whisked away, stretchered and unmoving through the emergency theatre doors and everyone wearing green masks except her. She remembered sitting on a vinyl seat in the waiting room. The lovely lady doctor emerged out of surgery, after four hours of saving an amazing woman's life. She was on first name terms with Seraphina now and emerged from the theatre smiling.

'She'll live.'
Seraphina hugged her in a merry dance. 'Oh you genius woman. Thank you from the bottom of my heart, dear Tess.'
'How's Mr Miracle?'
'Completely divine and utterly gorgeous.'
They both laughed and Seraphina told Tess about the hoped for reunion of E.B. with her long lost husband Davey.
'Are you kiddin' me?'
Seph shook her head 'Nope.'
'Well I'll be' beamed Tess.
'Jake's flying him home from Washington as we speak, and they'll be here later this morning.'
'Well, Ole E.B. is gonna be in intensive care for a while, that bullet went clean through her, shattering the base of her collar-bone, missing her throat and spine by millimeters and her heart by an inch or two. She's lost a whole lake o' blood and we'd better pray for no infection.'
'Pray ... Say ... heck it's all the same in the end. If E.B. was meant to die she'd most probably have died last night.'
'Yup.'
Tess looked at Seraphina, that fascinating woman from Wales whom she'd gladly got to know so well. 'You break me up, you know that?'
'Really?' said Miss Miraculous, as Tess took her left hand in hers and examined the exquisite diamond on her wedding finger with that instrument doctors use to peer into ears.
'Now that is what I call a result,' smiled Tess.

Seraphina was allowed a short moment with E.B. in the dawn light of an intensive care room.

E.B. looked peaceful and almost smiling despite all the bandages and monitors whirring and beeping around her. Clasping her friend's hand, it was a relief to feel its warmth. Confident that E.B. would recover, Seraphina slipped outside and took a deep breath, the scent of the Texas Hill Country was all around her and she inhaled deeply. The back of her neck tingled, and a warm, complete smile lit up her tired face as the super-clean, super-fresh, intense musky scent magically rejuvenated her, as it always did.

The town Sherriff was waiting for a statement and wanted to know if she was going to press charges against Mr Peterson. She didn't need to think about it and had decided she wouldn't, provided E.B. agreed. She reckoned Mr Peterson was having some kind of mid-life crisis and the gold fever had sent him over the edge, temporarily, she hoped. Anyway, without Mr Peterson, they most probably would never have become aware that Cutter's gold existed at all, and even now no one knew exactly what they were going to find at the bottom of the hole in the rock. As for the burning down of her house, the shrine to Gabe, it was for the best she now felt. It was dramatic and traumatic but necessary for her, so she could move forward and open her heart to the rest of her life. Danny, the town Sheriff, was glad he could let Mr Peterson go, he'd known him his whole life and confided in

Seraphina that the man had not been himself for a long time, since his wife had died after a long illness. 'Hell Danny, that's just awful ... poor man.
Danny went on, 'His two kids are twins and both wanting to go to college, he just needed the money, I'm guessing, and went stark staring crazy worrying about it ... I don't know.'
'I tell you what Danny, Cutter wanted his gold to be put to good use so depending on what we find down there maybe his kids can have the first two scholarships courtesy of ... ummm ... let me think... The Cutter Foundation.' Danny smiled from ear to ear. 'Gimme Five, Miss Cody! Gimme Five!'
The Sherriff went on to explain that his police officers were down at the bluff keeping watch over the scene and that forensics were going to drop a camera down the hole to find out if there was in fact any gold to be reclaimed. Ok that's great, right now I need to get back, it's still early and I have the ranch chores to do' said Seph, thanking the Sherriff.

By the time Seraphina got back to Turtle Creek Ranch it was around six in the morning, and she had time to check on the animals and go on over to E.B.'s and check on her little spread. The cell phone rang and it was Jake, he and Uncle Davey had just arrived at Chicago Airport and were about to climb aboard their connecting flight to San Antonio, before the drive home to the Hill Country. Hearing Jake's voice was a joy to Seraphina and she told him all about how E.B. got shot and the gold and Mr Peterson and that E.B. was alright. 'I love you Seph and need your kisses ... d'you hear me ..' said Jake and they laughed. 'Me too.. you gorgeous hunk of a thing ..' It turned out that Uncle Davey, E.B.'s long lost husband, was in pretty good shape despite having been a POW in Vietnam all those years ago. In his seventies now he could remember Twine Ranch and his beloved wife E.B., but he was a bit sketchy on most everything else. Jake said he was full of humour and the doctors believed he would adapt well to being reunited with his wife, bearing in mind he'd been somewhat institutionalized. Seraphina was intrigued, and wanted the full story. When Jake had cornered the woman who had been stalking E.B. she explained that she had been sent to track down Davey's wife, that Davey had requested it because he wanted to come home. Jake had been shocked at the news and saddened by the story. Davey had suffered unspeakably as a POW and the experience had left him shattered, disorientated and with no self-confidence, a shadow of his former self. The day when he returned home to surprise E.B. he was simply not equipped to deal with his utter devastation at finding her married to someone else, even though he knew everyone had mourned his death and had painfully moved on. It had been three years after all. So Davey had fled to Canada where he slowly rebuilt his life and he too had remarried, and lived a quiet existence on a small ranch. The years went by, his wife passed away, the ranch was sold and he was moved to a care home for the elderly. It was only when a young care-worker had cajoled him into talking about his life that the story of his broken heart was revealed. The care worker persuaded him to seek out his beloved wife with her help and Davey had happily agreed.

A quiet retirement with his long-lost wife on beautiful Twine Ranch seemed to be just the ticket for Uncle Davey, a lifestyle he was longing to restart. He'd kept on at his nephew Jake, on the flight out of Washington, about how he was looking forward to seeing his horses again. Jake didn't quite know how to explain that Socks, Marney and Floritta were long gone, dead. Davey was in some kind of happy time-warp and Jake was captivated, intrigued,

and hoped E.B. would feel the same way. The reunion was going to be quite something and there was no telling how it would go, how E.B would react, how Davey would be.

Seraphina was blown away by the story and dying to finally meet Uncle Davey. Jake kissed his gorgeous Seph goodbye on the phone and they agreed to meet up at the hospital around eleven that morning.

Seraphina called her friends at Tierra Cindy and was glad to hear they were all in one piece as she thanked them for their unwavering back-up and zest for getting stuck in when asked. The Unrestricted Ones were contacted too and were mightily relieved to hear that E.B. would live and were glad to have helped, glad to have been a part of all the drama the night before. Nat, Mabel, Max, Ruby, Tom and wonderful Straight Knee Standing were already planning the welcome home party at The Drover.

Seraphina's beloved Max was glad to see his mistress that morning. For his own protection he'd been shut in at E.B.'s house all night and was ecstatic at her arrival, leaping up and licking her and jumping all over the place. Seraphina took a quick shower and washed her hair before putting on clean Wranglers and her best boots. A crisp, white tucked-in shirt showed off her long-term tan, and her beautiful, strong short-nailed hands, so feminine and made for the single diamond decoration she now wore and never took off. She loved her engagement ring and adored having her wedding finger taken up, booked, bagged for good. 'Yes!' she exclaimed, twirling in front of the mirror and actually conceding that she wasn't bad for thirty-something. 'Lookin' good, feelin' good' and she danced around the room with Max.

They hopped in the truck and headed back to Turtle Creek Ranch, Seraphina needed to touch base with the men rebuilding the little house.

'Mornin' Seraphina',

'Hi Michael, don't mind the big bull-dozer parked up against the barn.'

'Okey Dokey, I won't ask, then.'

'It's a long story .. I'll explain when I get back.'

The cell phone rang and it was Tim from the drilling company.
'Hello Miss Cody, I called as soon as I got your message, you're
ready for us to un-cap that water hole right?'
'No not exactly .... I need you to do something else for me and keep it under your hat if you can.'
'Go on ...', Seraphina then went on to explain that she needed their expert dynamiting skills to retrieve some gold from solid rock. 'Ok .... you been drinkin', Miss Cody?'
'No no ... I'm deadly serious ... honestly.'
'I guess me and the boys could come on by and take a look.'
'Perfect ... thanks Tim, see you later then.'
She relaxed and got comfy in the truck seat and concentrated on driving back to town, Max riding in the back of the open pick-up enjoying the wind in his gold-dusted hair. She had an hour or so to spare before meeting up with Jake and Uncle Davey at the hospital, so she took a little detour into the Droversville Stockyards next door. There was activity everywhere and horses whinnying like mad. The livestock auction had begun and she strolled in with Max on a lead on his best pedigree behaviour, with people drawn to him and patting his head admiringly. The cattle sale almost done, next for the ring were the horses. A horse sale for Seraphina was like a big, giant treat. Her love of horses, her knowledge

of them and her passion for 'making' a good little horse, added to the extreme excitement of actually choosing one and putting her hand up to bid. Unlike everyone else, who studied the animals' conformation and teeth and how they walked and trotted and acted, Seraphina would simply stand close to the rails of the auction ring and every time a horse passed, she closed her eyes and 'sensed'. It was that 'sensation', 'feeling' that determined her decision. If she got a fluttering feeling in the pit of her stomach, she put her hand up to bid before even opening her eyes to see what she was hoping to acquire. Her gut feeling never failed and was the key to how she handled a horse, rewarded every time by the animal, who was all gut feeling and instinct, that's what made a horse such a special creature, to her mind. Her knack was to preserve the horse's confidence in his own natural instinct and to then ask, politely, if he wouldn't mind adding to his wild vocabulary, if she showed him how. She never 'broke' a horse, all she ever did was trust one. Eight hundred dollars later, she left the stockyards with a two-year-old filly with three and a half white socks and a smudged star on her beautiful face. Amber chestnut with a black mane and tail, a designer colour scheme if ever there was one. Stunning, pretty, intelligent and very pleased with the fun of being taken on a lead rein out of the stockyards, and round and round the car park by a nice lady.

'Ummm ... I'd really prefer it if you didn't do that right now ...' spoke Seraphina to the dancing, potty horse leaping all over the place and showing her two-tone belly as she stood on her hind legs. 'And no .... whinnying like that is not going to do it for me either ...'
'Hey lady! You need some help?' It was Jake and Uncle Davey, smiling at the spectacle of a beautiful woman and a beautiful horse getting to know each other on a sunny September morning in a busy car park. 'Yee Haa!' laughed Seraphina. 'Just couldn't resist, Jake .. just couldn't resist!'
'She's lovely, Seph ... not as lovely as you but lovely nevertheless!' and with that Jake kissed Seraphina slowly and passionately with a small cheering crowd and a dancing horse as the backdrop to their romantic reunion. Jake turned to introduce his Uncle Davey to his beautiful fiance and a helpful stranger indicated that he'd gone 'that away', pointing to the entrance of the stock yard housing the auction ring. Jake went after him quickly and Seraphina followed with Diamond, her newly christened horse. The three of them stood and scanned the lofty, dusty shed, Jake and Seph looking for Uncle Davey, and Diamond looking for trouble.
'If you do that one .... more ..... time ..', said Seraphina, through gritted teeth. 'You need to learn some manners, young lady, showing your belly like that in a public place, it's not ladylike.'
The filly was not letting up and Seraphina couldn't abide a horse who trod on her feet,

especially when she was wearing her best boots. Diamond was tottering on her hind legs, and shoving Seraphina, and putting her ears back, and generally having a fine old time. Someone was bidding on a horse in the ring and there was a Chinese whisper of excitement as two individuals fought it out, dollar by dollar .... a bidding war was on! The little crowd was caught up in the suspense, until finally the hammer went down and the auctioneer decreed: 'Sold! To the gentleman with the big cigar!'

'Uncle Davey smokes big cigars ...' said Jake to Seph.

'Ooops ....' said Seph to Jake.

Jake headed off into the crowd to recapture Uncle Davey and pay for a horse that he had a funny feeling his favourite long-lost Uncle now owned. Left alone with Diamond, Seraphina got up close and personal. 'Right then, poppet .... you and I are going to have a little chat .... in that round-pen over there ....' She took on a calm demeanour and confident stride, leading Diamond into the borrowed space. She only needed three and a half minutes – the maximum attention span of a young, feisty horse. The filly was all over the place and once safely inside the round-pen, Seraphina released the clip on the lead rein and Diamond hurtled off like a wild horse with nowhere to go, bucking and whinnying. Seraphina stood in the middle of the small arena and pinged the end of the lead rope at Diamond's rump, getting her, in a millisecond,

to canter free in a neat circle. Next, she stopped the filly dead in her tracks with another strategic ping of the rope and had her turn the other way, cantering in a different direction, leading with a different leg, hard work for Diamond who was puffing and licking her lips and dropping her head for the first time that day. Seraphina read the signals and turned her back on Diamond, stock still and waited, arms folded, in the middle of the space. A soft sorry nudge was quick in coming from the filly, who proceeded to follow Seraphina like a little lamb, whichever way she turned. The two of them joined forces that moment, having come to an agreement that it was better to be a part of the herd, even if it was just the two of them and Miss Miraculous clipped the lead rein back on to the head collar and off they went, Diamond now good as gold.
Meanwhile, Jake had located Uncle Davey and paid $2000.00 for a great little Paint Horse, five years old and beautifully trained in the art of everything by a much respected cowboy, Short Simon. Jake was well known at Droversville Stockyards, and that morning a large consignment of Twine Ranch Cattle had been sold for top dollars. His Ranch Foreman was there and glad to see Jake and Seraphina and Uncle Davey and two new horses. At last Jake was able to introduce Uncle Davey to Seraphina, and soon they were all laughing and drinking cowboy coffee and chatting about the newly acquired horses.

Jake's Comanche Foreman, Walks With A Smile, headed off with Boulder, the new Paint Horse, and Diamond the little novice, to load them into the big Twine Ranch trailer and drop Diamond off at Turtle Creek Ranch before heading back home to Twine Ranch with Boulder.

Jake and Seraphina were sitting either side of Uncle Davey on some straw bales in the crowded auction. They were both moved by the look of him, so frail, enjoying his cigar. His face in repose was lined and sad, his eyes were guarded, yet full of soul and the pain of human, inhuman suffering. His body was hunched and his once strong hands trembled. He had difficulty walking, one foot awkward to balance on and he used a cane. Seraphina fought back tears with all her might as she shook his hand and congratulated him on a horse well bought. She and Jake rallied round the old war veteran, desperate to protect him at this momentous time in his life.

'We'll take him to see E.B., Jake, and then we'll get him home, where he can be quiet.' Jake nodded agreement and they gently took an arm each and walked him to the truck for the few hundred yards' drive to the hospital.

Eleven o'clock and they were hopeful that E.B. would be conscious enough to meet Davey, her beloved husband, and that the emotion wouldn't be too much for either of them. 'Well here goes …' said Uncle Davey and in he went, to the bedside of his wounded long-lost wife. Jake and Seraphina waited in the corridor, giving the couple time alone. They kissed, and wondered with baited breath at the outcome of the tender meeting of loving souls behind the closed doors. A good twenty minutes passed before Davey beckoned them in to see E.B. She looked incredible, with a pretty feminine smile and contented aura, masking her difficulty breathing and the pain she was in. Holding Davey's hand tenderly, steadying the trembling, she asked Seraphina a question.

'Davey says he's bought me a lovely horse ... is that right?'

'Yes .. he sure has, E.B. … Boulder ... a real lady's horse ... turns on a sixpence ... light as a feather .... with great little 'handles'.'

'Why thank you, Davey of mine, I'm quite delighted, I must say.'

Davey kissed his wife and told her he loved her, moved to tears.

'Seph? Jake? Take good care of Boulder while I'm in here, it'll be a while before I can ride him so don't you go lettin' him get fat now!' murmured E.B. They all laughed and a solemn promise was made that Boulder would be cared for, as the very special gift that he undoubtedly was.

Chapter Twenty One

It was Thanksgiving and the perfect day to hold the house-warming party for Gabe's artisan cabin. Everything was rebuilt and finished and lovely, there was even proper electricity now, safely and legally installed at last. Seraphina had enjoyed the extraordinary pleasure, the night before, of sleeping in the house alone and cooking a nostalgic beef casserole in the tiny wood-fired oven, restored after the fire. The November weather was much cooler, prompting the lighting of both fires in both stone hearths in the double-cabin. 'Wow, awesome..' exclaimed Seraphina, getting grilled in front of huge crackling logs, then running outside to watch the smoke twirling out of the chimneys. 'Oh what is it about this place ... that is just so captivating?' she wondered, smiling and not really seeking the answer. From the back porch, she could see the floral meadow was wearing its late autumnal carpet of mainly green now, except for a tiny sprinkling of Blackfoot Daisies, pristine in their whiteness and jaunty, with their tiny bright yellow centres, a fitting natural decoration on the grave of Gabe's favourite horse.

She rode Diamond that evening in the cool, scented dusk of her beautiful little world, walking and talking to the pretty horse. Diamond was skittish and young, not intended for hard riding until maturity at five. This was her last outing with Seraphina astride to consolidate the lessons they had learned together before the mare would

be turned out for the Winter, so she could relax and get to grips with being a proper horse. The next Spring, Diamond would be reunited with Seraphina and they would continue the equine tutorials and build on the wonder of a horse's natural talents. 'Hey you .... cut it out ... ok?' Diamond was bouncing and jogging and Seraphina was wanting her to stretch her legs and walk out nicely. The mare had a soft sensitive mouth and pulling on it was a poor option, so Seraphina had replaced the steel bit with a rawhide bridge and it worked well, helping the horse to keep a chewing, salivating relationship to the gentle pressure and asked-for obedience. It took fifteen minutes of patient persuasion to get Diamond to use her gorgeous round quarters to power from behind and to walk balanced and square, the 'Alexander Technique' of Cowboys and Indians and Vaqueros since time began.
'Good girl .... Diamond ... and on that note we'll call it day.'
Seraphina dismounted and chatted to the little horse as she led her back to the holding paddock for the night. 'Now tomorrow Jake is coming to collect you and take you over to Twine Ranch ..... he's fixed it so you get to run with a hundred mares and have the freedom of a thousand acres ..' The mare snickered as though she understood, and Seraphina gently tugged on one silken ear.

It had been almost two months since E.B. had been rushed to hospital with the gun-shot wound and she was doing well, now back at Twine Ranch, walking and talking and spending most of her time with her beloved long-lost husband Davey. She cared for him and he cared for her, his frailty upstaged by his delightful take on life, his joy at being reunited with E.B. and his almost forgotten life on Twine Ranch.

Seraphina had been staying at E.B.'s while her house was getting finished and she and Jake spent romantic evenings there, in privacy, building on their wonderful love and getting to know one another. Seraphina would be moving to Twine Ranch after the Spring wedding. She and Jake loved the fact that they lived separately for now, it was an old fashioned courtship and their time together was utterly heavenly and never taken for granted. They both looked glowing and young, and they made a handsome, loving couple. Jake spent money on his beautiful woman, custom spurs and hand-made cowboy boots, understated and chic as hell. She wore engraved silver ear-rings and a necklace, all crafted especially for her, by the lovely artisan jewellery maker at Twine Ranch. The prettiest pair of deer skin 'chinks' were her most favourite thing, knee-length chaps with long fringes and beaded on the front in the loveliest manner – Comanche beadwork to cherish – tiny hand-stitched work created by Walks With A Smile's wife. The pink and lilac beads set off against the 'tobacco' tanned deer skin, super soft and heavy. Seraphina was kept busy and happy running Turtle Creek Ranch and setting up The Cutter Foundation, a gift of a thing that she would use for the good of a lot of people. The final count valued the gold treasure at just under a million dollars. What a day that was and everyone would remember it and future generations would hear of it. The borehole boys had turned up that day, as requested, and worked out quickly where to drill and where to set off a small explosion to open up the hole in the rock and retrieve the cache of old stashed bags, Theobald's haul of gold from more than a century ago.

It was a great task and required a make-shift containment in case the gold got blown into the stratosphere, so reinforcements were drafted in and a camp was set up down by the bluff. There was hilarious fun for all, a cook-out mustered and a night under the stars, preparing for the following morning. Huge sheets and tarpaulins had been borrowed and between the many willing hands they were able to enclose the soon-to-be-blown-up rock in a voluminous tent, held in place by anything to hand. The happy band was full of anticipation at how successful they may or may not be in the unusual circumstances. The crew stayed the night at the foot of the tall bluff and they made a wonderful, delicious supper over a campfire, Nat and Mabel and Viper and Hellfire dishing out portions on old tin plates. Scorpion and Ice had brought their guitars and entertained everyone with old haunting cowboy songs, describing a life on a long cattle drive, verse after verse, word perfect and an education in themselves. The fire was kept just so by Straight Knee Standing who was looking forward to lighting a pipe later on and sitting with his friends smoking in peace. Drinks were above and beyond a usual cowboy fare. Tom had mustered a range of zinging cocktails with crushed ice, umbrellas and all the trimmings including cherries and lemons and sprigs of fresh mint. Seats had been arranged around the campfire by Chilli One and Blue, old logs with blankets thrown over them were just the ticket and everyone sat comfortably, eating and drinking and star-watching and having a special time. Chilli Two and Mixer had set out a single picnic table and tablecloth with a candle and flowers and two camp chairs a little way away from the others and had insisted that Jake and Seraphina have dinner in the romantic setting and splendour of the place as the two 'lovebirds' of the group, which they did. The two of them like guests in a fine restaurant in a virtual outdoors, only this was real. Jake looked at Seraphina and felt the same deep emotional response he always did when she was near, and instinctively touched her cheek with his hand and tidied a strand of her hair, which had fallen loose from the ribbon tying it back. There was something about Seraphina, a fragility which drew attention because her presence moved those who came in contact with her. The way she stood, the way she talked, the way she looked in repose when she thought she was alone. A showing of who she was. Her prettiness had been a blight to her, in a way, all her life. Unwittingly seductive as a young woman, attracting attention from people who didn't really care or worse. Men who took her as a trophy and betrayed. Women who were jealous and damaging. Part of the reason she loved her thirties and the inevitable progress of middle-age to old, was because her depreciating looks meant she was more valued. The greying hair meant she was taken seriously, if she wanted it. The thin lines beginning to show on her face stopped shallow attentions in their tracks. Any young buck or decrepit one for that matter, would think twice before aiming to use her. Her attractiveness was there all right, bolstered now by the face of experience, a life filled out by reality and survival. She had matured into a whole person and was no longer sitting on the dross of emotional damage and grief, instead everything was in its place now – time being the ultimate healer. Time was a hard task master too, the business of waiting to recover from loss and smashed dreams not to mention injury, could be slow yet giving of a reward – relief from suffering.

Sitting opposite Jake in the moonlight eating and laughing, Seraphina breathed a deep wonderful sigh, she had finally moved on, and was overjoyed, calm, loved, her equilibrium restored.

Next day at dawn, everyone was issued with hard hats and gathered at the foot of the bluff to hang on to the flapping plastic sheeting. The detonator was set and the final countdown began.... ' Five ... four ... three ... two ... one BOOM!!!!!' It literally rained gold that day, pockets were filled with it, boots were smothered in it, lungs breathed it in with choking hilarity, great lumps of solid gold bounced off hard hats and the tumbling and rumbling of people and the precious golden metal in all its unminted variance made a sight like no other. The mission had been a success and the rest of the day was spent bagging it all up before a police escort arrived to ferry it for valuation to the local bank vault.

The Cutter Foundation was established and great plans lay ahead to use Turtle Creek Ranch as a centre for respite, for individuals to come and stay and let the environment work its magic on them. Mr Petersen's kids got their special scholarships to get them through college and Seph used the rest to restore the native grass meadows which had blown away half a century before. Last but not least, Mr Miracle had been tested for his genetic blueprint and it transpired he was as close to the original wild bison that had once existed, before they were hunted to near extinction, as anyone could have hoped for. His new role in life was about to begin as the bull buffalo sire of a hoped for brand new herd. The

Yellowstone National Park had agreed to send a pair of good breeding female buffalo for Mr Miracle and Seraphina was thrilled.
There was the wedding of Seraphina and Jake to look forward to and a whole beautiful new adventure opening up. Spurred on by her new-found wealth, Seraphina had taken on extra local workmen to speed up the completion of Gabe's cabin, and the whole thing was finished well ahead of Christmas. November Thanksgiving was the date set for a wonderful celebration and house-warming party. Seraphina's Mum and Dad were to be whisked to Texas, and the 'clecs' burnt a trail through the little Welsh market town when the news got out. Seraphina paid for all her friends in Wales to fly out and have a pre-Christmas holiday of a lifetime. Rosey, Juliette , Neil and Cath, Lewis and his wife, were all sent tickets. Seraphina had already mentioned to Jake that neither Rosey or Juliette were married and both were horse mad and that maybe a little Texas matchmaking might be in order. Jake twinkled at the prospect and mentally lined up Buck and Lester, two of his trusted crew, who were about ready to find the right women and settle down.
E.B. and Davey were given the task of picking out twenty good horses from Twine Ranch so that all the guests could ride out each day with Jake and Seraphina watching over them. E.B. and Davey were amazing, resilient to all that had happened to them, powered by a passion for life and their great love for one another, reunited at

last. They spent the happiest days getting to know each other again, putting Jake's horses through their paces, ensuring that only the quiet ones were sent over to Turtle Creek Ranch in the big trailer. Three extra round pens were built to corral all the extra livestock, and Betsy and Leopold were very uppity about the whole thing, hurtling around the flat meadow with their tails in the air, pretending to be horses. 'You two old muley things, have a sugar lump and calm down. You both know that we all love that you're mutants, it makes you very special.' Seraphina was standing at the fence rail with Leopold resting his whiskery lips on top of her head and breathing heavily, and Betsy was nibbling Leopold's big old waggly ear. 'Now you two, in a few days all our guests will be arriving from Wales, and I'm counting on you to be on your best behaviour, ok?' The mules responded by galloping off and kicking their heels in the air, as if to say, 'When Hell freezes over' making Seraphina smile at the sight of them, proud of the delinquents she had inherited, glad of their extreme, unstinting willfulness.

It was amazing to see what money and goodwill can do. Within a couple of weeks an extra bunk house had been built, new bathrooms installed, beds, curtains, sofas, and a little cantina had been created, all out of logs and sheer happy human endeavour. The Cutter Foundation was getting well and truly inaugurated. Mum and Dad arrived safely. The landscape blew them away as Jake swept them off in his luxurious cowboy truck for the journey from San Antonio Airport, each mile taking them closer to the heart of the Texas Hill Country and their cherished daughter, who was waiting at the ranch. They marvelled at the lilting vistas and loved the scent of juniper in the air. The blue, blue sky took their breath away and they held hands and pinched each other, to make sure they weren't dreaming. Seraphina's joy at seeing her Mum and Dad was only capped by the pet's joy as Max and Mr Miracle chased them round and round the outside of the house before they'd even had a chance to hug their precious daughter.

Next up, the goats broke loose. Cricket, Mirabelle and Mitzi the Kid set about rummaging in Mum's handbag and Dad's big overcoat pockets, before skipping off with trophies – a packet of Extra Strong Mints, Mum's reading glasses and Dad's passport. Seraphina steered her parents into the house and shut the livestock out. Laughing and hugging, they watched through the window as Jake sprinted after the goats wielding a coiled rope so expertly that he captured the renegades within seconds. Out of breath, he came back to the house having retrieved the spectacles and passport with only superficial teeth marks. The mints were never recovered and the goats had the freshest breath in Texas.

Mum and Dad just couldn't take it all in, the sheer joy of the world they had just stepped into and the beauty of the environment made them laugh with excitement – they felt young again and without a hint of jet-lag. Jake took his future father-in-law off to Droversville to get him kitted out in Gentleman's cowboy attire, and they had the best time trying on Stetsons. Mum and Seraphina got baking and produced mounds of delicious Welsh cakes and a big pot of 'cawl', a fragrant Welsh dish of clear, glistening beef stew infused with fresh parsley and white pepper. Halcyon days followed, her friends from Wales arrived and Turtle Creek Ranch was a hive of activity and cooking and laughter and hilarious outings on horse-back. One outing in particular was organized by Seraphina. At daybreak on Thanksgiving Day she had every single guest mounted on steeds of every shape and size – it was like Thelwell meets Bonanza. 'Ok everyone let's move out,' and off they went. Mum, Dad, E.B., happy and resplendent on Boulder, her new horse – her long-lost husband's precious gift. Straight Knee Standing, Amy and Jake Jnr., Nat, Mabel, Tom, all the troop from Tierra Cindy, Tess the lovely lady doctor who'd saved E.B.'s life, Michael and the boys who'd rebuilt everything in record time, Seraphina's friends from Wales and Tim and the borehole crew. Juliette and Rosey were special childhood friends of Seph, they had grown up together riding scruffy Welsh ponies in the gorgeous Welsh countryside and their reunion was a joy to behold, so much laughter their sides ached.

Unbeknown to everyone, Jake and Seraphina had organized a surprise breakfast cook-out of pancakes and maple syrup and ham and eggs, and steaming fresh ground coffee, and just when the guests were too polite to say they were freezing with sore backsides, their collective nostrils flared at the exquisite aroma of hot, fresh-cooked breakfast on the open range. Capable Chuey, the son of Reina, Jake's Mexican housekeeper at Twine Ranch was a vision in white. Dressed like a professional chef, he stood over a smoking mesquite fire, with a table nearby complete with condiments and china plates. Boy, they tucked in and well and truly experienced 'a great time had by all'. Jake was kissing Seraphina and she was kissing him back, when a nudge on her shoulder interrupted proceedings. She turned to look, and there before her were Leopold and Betsy in full harness with the open wagon in tow. 'Are you kiddin' me?' she looked at Jake for back up. 'Don't look at me, Seph, I've got nothing to do with this, right Chuey?' 'Right, Uncle Jake,' said Chuey, one of the finest horsemen in all of Texas. He went on, "O.K., all those wishing to experience a winter morning wagon ride back to the ranch house, climb aboard!' Seraphina's Mum and Dad clambered up into the old wood wagon, excited at the prospect of yet another novel experience, next followed by almost everyone and off they went, Leopold and Betsy walking slowly and stopping whenever Chuey asked them. The Tierra Cindy troop gingerly walking on foot alongside, casually but emphatically remarking that they preferred terra firma.

'Well I'll be ... how the hell did Chuey do that ... get my mules to walk slowly and stop when asked?' Jake just hugged his beautiful woman and chuckled as she broke free and started chasing him round and round the camp fire. 'Hell Seph... I love you ... it's not your fault you can't control a pair of old mules!' 'What? Just you wait 'til I get a hold of you!' She couldn't catch him and gave up, laughing and out of breath, collapsed on the ground by the camp fire. A divine lingering kiss left her speechless, and Jake loved that he had that effect on her, and so did Seraphina.

A cloud of dust and the sound of galloping hooves heralded the arrival of Jake's matchmaking efforts, which he'd taken seriously enough to organize thoroughly. Rosey and Juliette were waving from the back of the mule wagon when Buck and Lester, both eligible men, rode up alongside and introduced themselves, tipping their hats, followed swiftly with an invitation to go dancing one evening. Juliette was captivated by Lester and Buck was captivated by Rosey, Jake had done his job well and the new foursome chatted easily and confidently, all of them smiling, knowing they were probably, definitely, going to have some fun.

Seph sighed a sigh of satisfaction seeing her childhood friends flirting for the first time in a long

while and knowing they were in good hands, with good men.
She and Jake took all the saddles and bridles off the horses and let them run free for the rest of that special day. The horses took off at a gallop, bucking and squealing and made a powerful sight looping in a perfect arc and off and away into the big meadow. After loading the heavy saddles onto the truck Chuey had parked, they put the camp fire out, collected all the dishes and plates, and headed back to the ranch. They arrived ahead of the others who'd taken the long way round in the old wagon, and washed up before setting the tables for the Thanksgiving party later that day.
An hour or so passed before everyone arrived safely back at the ranch, and Betsy and Leopold weren't even sweating, just calmly waggling their ears at Seraphina, who looked at them in puzzlement, while Chuey and Jake winked at one another.
Her sister Lauren and brother-in-law Patrick, travelling from Marlborough, England, still hadn't arrived yet and Seph was getting anxious, they should have been there by now. A call to Frank, the cab driver she'd sent to the airport to collect them, gave her the reason why, they'd insisted on being dropped at the bottom meadow so they could stretch their legs and walk the last mile to the house. 'Oh no Frank .. Dozer the bull is down there and he'll be bored by now, just looking for something or someone to chase!' Jake heard the conversation and sent Buck and Lester careering

off on horseback to rescue her sister and husband. Lauren and Patrick were spotted running in frantic zig-zags with Dozer trundling after them, head down, horns pointing the way straight to Patricks' backside. Dozer was old and cronky which was a blessing, he could still put on a show but did everything at half-speed nowadays, and just when Lauren covered her eyes because she couldn't bear to watch, Buck lifted her off the ground and onto his horse all at a full gallop. Next Lester diverted the angry old bull, giving Patrick time to scramble up a tree, then when he was sure Dozer had lost interest he came back and gave Seph's brother-in-law a ride back to the house, 'Welcome to Texas Patrick … mighty pleased to meet you… sorry for the bumpy start.' Poor Patrick was speechless, he was an advertising executive, very particular about his clothes, and unused to an outdoor life. The newly arrived couple received a heroes welcome and Seraphina hugged them to death before dusting them off and removing bits of twig from what had been, their immaculate hairdos. E.B. was first in line to shake Patricks' hand and complemented him on the scent of his aftershave, 'Umm Paco Raban, I'd recognize it anywhere.' Patrick was pleased, and in his impeccable clipped, upper-class British accent replied, 'I take it you work in fragrance Eve, splendid you must tell me all about it.' E.B. winked at Seraphina and politely showed the new guests to their room.

Mum and Dad were nowhere to be seen and Seph went to find them to give them the good news that their other daughter had arrived safely. She tracked them down in the barn standing over a wooden crate which Jake and Seraphina had brought back from a San Antonio auction. The crate was full of old sepia framed photos., bought as a job-lot to decorate the walls at Turtle Creek. The auctioneer describing them as a 'time-capsule from the days of early settlers' Mum was looking intently at one of the pictures, Dad peering hard too. It showed two men proudly holding a set of deer antlers above their heads, a Comanche Chief stood to their right with a Comanche woman and child in the foreground, the backdrop was just visible and showed a river chock-block with logs, 'Well, well, well,' said Mum, 'That's your Uncle Morgan and Uncle Huw, and I expect that must be White Cloud.' Seraphina couldn't believe her ears and looked carefully at the splendid photograph, recognizing with an added beat of her heart, that it was the Warrior Chief she'd encountered in her strange dream the day that Gabe's house had been destroyed.

She was overwhelmed with a sense of knowing she was where she ought to be, where she wanted to be, yet humbled by the sheer scale of the synchronicity that had brought her to this point in her life.

She closed her eyes for a moment in thankfulness and contentment, knowing she was where she belonged and glad that whatever else happened in her glorious life, ultimately her last words would be: 'Scatter my ashes at Turtle Creek' and she would die happy.

Also by Sara Llewellyn - Earth Meadow, a pictorial diary of her mother's Welsh childhood, curated original paintings and commentary.

About the Author: Sara has in turn been an actress with The Royal Shakespeare Company, a TV Presenter, a Texan land owner and a painter and furniture restorer. She lives in her beloved Wales, and dedicates Scatter My Ashes At Turtle Creek to her beloved son Alex.

****

For high quality prints of the Earth Meadow collection visit my online shop

At EarthMeadowPrints.Etsy.com

Follow on Facebook at Earth Meadow Art Prints